THREE LITTLE WORDS

"Rory?" Dean said.

"Yes?" I whispered, looking into his eyes.

Dean hesitated, then said softly, "I love you."

Everything stopped.

I blinked. I couldn't speak.

Dean waited expectantly, and when I still said nothing, his brow furrowed in concern. "Rory?" he prompted. "Did you hear me?"

"Uh huh."

"Well . . . say something."

"I . . ." I sat up a little. "I . . ."

"Yes?" He encouraged me, searching my face, staring into my eyes.

I turned away, glanced at the steering wheel, the dashboard. "I . . . I *love* the car!"

"That's . . . that's it?"

"No. I just . . . I'm surprised. I didn't expect . . . I don't . . ."

"You don't love me." He pulled his arm from around me and sat up straight.

"No! I-I just have to think for a minute."

"Think about *what*?"

"Well, saying 'I love you' is a really difficult thing."

"Well, I just did it."

"And you did it really well."

"What the hell does *that* mean?"

"I . . . please," I said. "This totally came as a surprise, I mean, the dinner, and the car, and then the . . . I just need a minute to think about it."

"This is not something that you think about, Rory!" he exclaimed. "This is something that you feel or you don't."

Other *Gilmore Girls* Books

LIKE MOTHER, LIKE DAUGHTER

Coming Soon

I DO, DON'T I?

Gilmore girls

I Love You, You Idiot

ADAPTED BY CATHY EAST DUBOWSKI
FROM THE TELEVISION SERIES CREATED BY
AMY SHERMAN-PALLADINO,
FROM THE TELEPLAY "THAT DAMN DONNA REED"
WRITTEN BY DANIEL PALLADINO
& AMY SHERMAN-PALLADINO,
THE TELEPLAY "CHRISTOPHER RETURNS"
WRITTEN BY DANIEL PALLADINO,
THE TELEPLAY "STAR-CROSSED LOVERS
AND OTHER STRANGERS"
BY JOHN STEPHENS & LINDA LOISELLE GUZIK,
STORY BY JOAN BINDER WEISS,
THE TELEPLAY "THE BREAK-UP, PART II"
WRITTEN BY AMY SHERMAN-PALLADINO,
THE TELEPLAY "P.S. I LO . . ."
WRITTEN BY ELAINE ARATA & JOAN BINDER WEISS,
AND THE TELEPLAY "LOVE, DAISIES AND TROUBADOURS"
WRITTEN BY DANIEL PALLADINO

HarperEntertainment
An Imprint of HarperCollinsPublishers

HARPERENTERTAINMENT
An Imprint of HarperCollins*Publishers*
10 East 53rd Street
New York, New York 10022-5299

ISBN: 0-06-050228-2

First HarperEntertainment paperback printing: July 2002

10 9 8 7 6 5 4 3 2 1

Gilmore girls

1

The world is black and white. Women wear huge skirts, pearls, red lipstick, and flipped hair that doesn't budge when the wind blows—and that's their casual at-home look when they're in the kitchen frying bacon and eggs. The children are all scrubbed and polite—the girls in perky pastel sweater sets and plaid skirts, the boys in neat dress shirts and slacks—and they say things like "Aw, jeepers, Mom" when they're *really* bummed out.

And every family has a calm, rational husband and father who comes home at the end of the day with a pipe, a briefcase, and a regular paycheck.

Mom and I were watching black-and-white reruns of—*The Donna Reed Show*. It's like a bizarre time capsule from the late fifties. A show that reflected—or maybe even instructed—post–World War II households on how the perfect American family looked, acted, spoke, and thought.

I glanced at my mom, Lorelai. She was slouched on

the couch, wearing a snug HEAVY METAL RULES T-shirt over a favorite pair of well-worn jeans.

At 32, she's only sixteen years older than I am and is often mistaken for my big sister. I'm an only child, so I wouldn't know for sure, but from what I've seen of other people and their siblings, I think I like her a lot better than that. We've been on our own since I was born and she's more than my mom—she's my best friend.

There was a knock at the door and a male voice called out, "Hello?"

"Did you come bearing pizza?" Mom called out.

"I'm not an idiot," the voice replied.

"Get in here!" she ordered.

In strolled my boyfriend, Dean. Tall and slim, dark-haired, and gorgeous, he brings the gift of dinner. Yes, he is the perfect boyfriend.

"Hey." I grinned up at him.

"Hey." He grinned back.

"Sit," Mom said, too engrossed in Donna to do the perfect hostess thing. "You're totally missing it."

Dean glanced at the TV as he came around to where I was sitting. "What are we watching?"

Mom beamed. "The true, totally incomparable *Donna Reed Show*."

Dean laid two large stacked pizza boxes on the coffee table. A brown paper bag sat on top of the boxes.

I peered at it curiously. "What's in there?"

Dean shrugged as he took off his black leather jacket and tossed it on a chair. "Salad."

"Salad?"

Dean nodded. "Yeah. It's a quaint dish, sometimes used to precede large quantities of pizza."

Mom and I stared at him.

Dean squirmed. "It's . . . for me?"

"Clearly," I said. Don't get me wrong. I eat salad. I like salad. Mom and I even have salad in the house occasionally. But tonight we had onions and green pepper on the pizzas, so we figured we had the vegetable thing covered.

Mom propped her feet on the coffee table and flipped open one of the boxes right on her lap. She handed me a slice and I took a bite, relishing the long strings of gooey cheese.

Dean sat down on the floor near me and dug into his salad. "So who's Donna Reed?" he asked.

"What?" I nearly dropped my pizza.

"You don't know who Donna Reed is?" Mom exclaimed. "The quintessential fifties mom—with the perfect fifties family?"

"Never without a smile and high heels?" I further clarified.

"Hair that if you hit it with a hammer, it would crack?" Mom explained.

Dean blinked. "So . . . it's a show?"

"It's a *lifestyle*," I said.

"It's a *religion*," Mom declared.

I wiped my mouth with a napkin. "My favorite episode—"

"Yes! Tell me, tell me!" Mom begged.

"—is when their son, Jeff, comes home from school . . . and *nothing happens*."

"Oh, that's a good one." Mom grinned at Dean. "One of my favorites is when Mary, the daughter, gets a part-time job . . . and *nothing happens*."

"Another classic," I agreed.

Dean pointed his plastic salad fork at the TV screen. "So what's this one about?"

Mom leaned forward. "Well, this one's actually full of intrigue. Her husband, Alex, comes home late for dinner"—she glanced sideways at me—"and he *didn't call*!"

I shook my head in mock disgust. "Might as well kick the dog too."

"Oh, oh, look!" Mom said, pointing at the TV. "She's making *doughnuts*!"

We watched a moment as Donna Reed's character—Donna Stone—made doughnuts with her son, Jeff.

"Hey, you're getting behind in the sugar department," Donna chirped.

"Oh, I guess I was thinking of something else, Mom," Jeff replied.

"Not that my sugary attitude wouldn't make anyone an instant diabetic," Mom quipped in an imitation of Donna's voice.

A moment later Donna and her teenage daughter, Mary, were on either side of the opened back door, still in their perfect clothes, scrubbing vigorously at the door's window panes.

"Mother-daughter window washing. We should try that," I remarked.

"Yes," Mom agreed. "Right after the mother-daughter shock treatments."

Then Mom and I took over the Donna Reed episode.

"You know, daughter, there's nothing more satisfying than washing the windows," Mom began. "Oh no!"

"What?" I gasped. "Did I miss a spot?"

"No. I just had an impure thought about your father, Alex. Funny, I don't know why I had it. It isn't the second Saturday of the month."

Enter Dr. Alex Stone, who popped his head in the kitchen window from the backyard. I lowered my voice. "Hey, I heard you had an impure thought about me!"

Mom was "distraught." "I must now sublimate all my impure thoughts by going into the kitchen and making an endless stream of perfect casseroles."

"You're not even listening to the dialogue!" Dean protested.

"Ours is better," I said.

Dean stared down into his salad, stirring croutons around in the remaining dressing. "I don't know . . . It all seems kind of nice to me."

"What does?" I asked.

He shrugged. "You know, families hanging together." He looked back at the TV. "I mean, a wife cooking dinner for her husband. And look—she seems really happy."

"She's medicated," Mom said.

"And acting from a script," I pointed out.

"Written by a *man*!" Mom exclaimed in mock outrage.

"Well said, Sister Suffragette!" I high-fived her.

But then I noticed that Dean wasn't laughing with us. "But what if she *likes* making doughnuts and dinner for her family and keeping things nice for them and . . ."

Mom and I just sat there, and stared at him.

Dean winced. "Okay, I feel very unpopular right now."

"No, no, I understand where you're coming from. I mean, you and Donna are kindred spirits. You both work in aprons," Mom teased, referring to Dean's attire at his part-time job at Doose's Market.

"Let's watch the show," he said, trying to shift the focus away from him.

"Oh, we're just having fun," I said.

"Um, okay. Eyes off me now," Dean replied, clearly regretting he said anything to begin with.

Then the perfect Donna interrupted.

"You know, dear," she cheerfully told her husband as she set yet another casserole on the table, *"the first ten years we were married, I was upset when you came home late for dinner."*

Dr. Stone looked surprised. *"You're not anymore?"*

"No," Donna said brightly. *"You are no longer late for dinner, you're just extremely early for breakfast."*

As the laugh track played, Dean squirmed. "Hey." He held up his hands. "I'm not saying a word."

2

The next morning, Mom and I headed to Luke's Diner in search of breakfast.

Luke's has the best breakfast in town. It's not always the easiest to find for people who don't live in Stars Hollow as the sign outside reads "Williams Hardware." Luke's dad used to own the place as a hardware store. When he died, Luke decided to turn it into a diner but he never changed the sign, which Mom thinks is really sweet. There are even some hardware odds and ends scattered about.

"Can brains hurt?" I asked as we walked through the door.

"Yes!" Mom said as we grabbed the nearest table. "It's hypochondria hour."

"I'm serious," I told her as I slid into my seat. "Last night, when I was reading my biology chapters, I distinctly heard a ping in the vicinity of my brain."

Mom took her seat. "Your brain pinged?"

"Yeah, it went like . . . *dink*."

"Well, then, honey, your brain *dinked*, it didn't *ping*."

"Well, I don't think a *dinking* brain is any less worrisome than a *pinging* brain."

"You got me there."

"So should I go to a tumor doctor?" I persisted.

"No, you don't have a tumor," Mom said. "You're reading too much. You're probably just losing your eyesight."

"Thank you."

"You're welcome."

Luke came over to take our order. Tall and rugged, about Mom's age, he almost always wears a plaid flannel shirt and jeans, his dark hair curling out from under a backward baseball cap. He didn't smile as he stopped at our table and pulled his order pad out of his back pocket.

If you didn't know him, you might think he was unfriendly. But he's really a nice guy. He and Mom have become pretty good friends lately.

Mom grinned at Luke in her usual cheerful way. "Hey, can you take some constructive criticism?"

Luke pulled a pencil from behind his ear. "No."

"Okay," she said cheerfully, undeterred, and proceeded as if he'd said, *Yes, please*. "This place could use a *makeover*," she announced.

Luke squinted at her. "Huh?"

"You know, a little sprucing up. A coat of paint . . ."

Luke shook his head. "I *don't spruce*."

"What do you mean, you don't *spruce*?"

The answer came from behind him, as a heavyset man in a cardigan sweater spun around on his stool at the counter. "What he means is he *won't* spruce. *That's* what he means."

Luke rolled his eyes. "Taylor—do not start."

But Taylor Doose, owner of Doose's Market, ignored the warning, his salt-and-pepper beard making him look like an outraged professor. "Me and the rest of the town beautification committee have been hounding him for years to freshen up the place, maybe put some nice zinnia pots outside, some yellow awnings . . . a peppy little cardboard pig announcing the special."

I traded looks with Mom—she was struggling not to burst out laughing.

"But he's a *mule*!" Taylor went on. "He won't talk, he won't reason, he *won't spruce*. You might as well forget it, Lorelai. I'm forgetting it too." He went back to eating.

"Finally," Luke said loud enough to be heard, "a Taylor Doose position I can get behind."

Taylor spun around again. "Faded paint is a bad reflection on the whole town!"

"Whatever happened to giving up?" Luke muttered.

"When standards slip, families flee," Taylor declared, "and in comes the seedy crowd. You got trouble, my friend—"

"Right here in River City!" Mom said, finishing a line from *The Music Man* as she slapped her hand on the table.

"This is not funny, Lorelai," Taylor scolded.

"Does anyone *want* anything?" Luke said, completely annoyed.

"Yes. I do," Mom said, serious again as she studied the menu. "I want . . . to know *why you won't paint this place*," she said in a rush, smiling up at him again.

Luke leaned forward. "Painting is a *pain*. I have to

close the place for a day, which I can't afford, or paint it in the middle of the night, which I don't want to do, because I *hate* painting."

"Okay, how about this? I'll help you." She beamed. "I *love* to paint."

Luke frowned. "You do."

"Yes, I do."

"You love it."

"I would like to *marry* it."

Luke shook his head. "You've got strange passions."

"She likes washing dishes too," I chimed in. "She's multifaceted abnormal."

"Ah, come on," Mom tried to convince him. "We'll drink a couple beers, we'll sing painting songs—"

"Painting songs," Luke repeated.

"Yeah, painting songs!"

Luke and I exchanged a dubious look as Mom continued. "You know, the one that goes, uh . . ." She started to sing, using her utensils to tap on her water glass as she made up some words. "Grab your brush and grab your rollers . . . all you kids and all you . . . bowlers . . . we're going a-paintin' today!" Mom sang with gusto.

Luke stared at her.

"Say yes or there's a second verse," Mom warned. She knows how to drive a hard bargain.

Luke sighed and glanced around the diner. "Well . . . I guess maybe, if I had help . . ."

Taylor Doose whirled on his stool again. "Really? Oh, my God! That's wonderful! Hur-*rah*!"

Luke gritted his teeth and didn't turn around. "Taylor, it's not for you, it's for me."

But Taylor was so excited he sprang from his stool.

"I can't wait to tell the rest of the committee! They're not going to believe this!" The bell on the door jangled as he dashed out into the street.

Luke watched him go. "I hate that he's pleased."

"Ah, you'll drop a gum wrapper on the street in front of his store later," Mom said.

Luke nodded. "Yeah, good idea."

I smiled as Luke took our orders, the *ping* in my brain forgotten.

That night we headed out, dressed and pretty, for our Friday night dinner at my grandparents' house. These weekly meals were a condition my grandmother placed on us when Mom asked to borrow money for Chilton when I first got in. I actually enjoy these gatherings because they've given me the chance to get to know my grandparents, plus, our dinners there are more elegant than any restaurant I've ever been in — white linen tablecloth, flowers, candles, wine and someone to cook and serve the meals. Mom doesn't always feel the same, but I do think she's starting to get used to them. She looked lovely as she took a sip from her wineglass.

"Kick ass wine."

"How poetic," Grandma responded sarcastically.

"It's got a nice smell," Mom went on. "Earthy. Vibrant. You can taste the Italian's feet."

"It's a Bordeaux," my grandfather corrected her. "It's French."

"Huh." Mom stared at the glass. "Well, what's an Italian's foot doing in a French wine?"

I could see where this was headed, so I tried to quickly change the subject.

"So when do you guys leave for Martha's Vineyard?" I asked.

"We're not going to Martha's Vineyard this year," Grandpa said.

"Really? Why not?"

"Our usual rental was unavailable when we inquired." He glared down the table at Grandma. "*Late.*"

"We should have just bought a place years ago, like I wanted," Grandma responded, tight-lipped.

"It wouldn't have been prudent," Grandpa replied.

"Now we have no place to go next week," Grandma complained.

"Well, you guys could always go somewhere else, couldn't you?" I suggested.

Grandpa looked astonished. "We always go to the Vineyard this time of year."

"You need to break the chain, Dad," Mom said. "Go to Paris."

"Yes, Paris!" I agreed.

"Impressionism. Poodles," Mom said.

"Crème brulée," I added.

Mom nodded. "Ooh, that's good."

"Impossible!" Grandpa stated.

"*Porquoi*?" Mom smiled at me. "French."

"We only go to Europe in the fall," Grandma explained crossly.

"You know, Mom, I heard a rumor that Europe's still there in the spring."

"I've heard that too," I said helpfully.

"We know it's there in the spring, but we never go in the spring because we always go in the fall."

"Okay, this is getting a little too Lewis Carroll for me," Mom muttered.

I listened to them argue back and forth some more as I ate my dinner.

"It costs a fortune to travel first class in Europe," Grandpa was saying. "We only do it every two years."

"In the fall," Grandma said.

"It's just not in the budget this year," Grandpa added.

"You don't have to travel first class," Mom said.

The room fell silent and Grandma, stopped with her fork halfway to her mouth, stared at Mom. Grandpa stared, too, his wineglass frozen in midair.

"'Cause . . . uh, there's always coach," Mom said.

My grandparents continued staring at her, horrified at the thought.

"Or . . . business class is slightly less." Mom rambled, trying to fill the silence. "There's deals on the Internet."

My grandparents looked at each other down the long table. "Pass the potatoes," Mom said, quickly trying to change the topic.

"You got it," I said.

⚮

Monday morning quickly rolled around and I was concentrating on history note cards in the kitchen while Mom tried to focus on the button she was trying to sew on on the cardigan of my school uniform. That's the one domestic surprise about Mom: she could sew Donna Reed under the table. You should see some of her amazing creations.

"Catherine the Great, 1729 to '96," I muttered, concetrating on my notecards, "Empress of Russia 1762 to '96 . . ."

"Okay. Hold still, please," Mom ordered.

"Originally named Sophie Fredericke August Von Anhalt-Zerbst . . ."

"But everybody called her kitten," Mom added.

"Married to Grand Duke Peter of Holstein in 1754 . . ."

"Okay, Rory, seriously . . ."

"Their marriage was an unhappy one," I went on.

"Well, there were way too many names," Mom replied.

I reached across the table for the rest of my cards.

"Ow!" Mom winced and stuck her thumb in her mouth. "Okay, lady with notecards look at lady with needle and just try to focus for one second so that I can sew the button on your sweater and not on my thumb."

"I'm sorry."

I started to go back to my notecards when someone knocked at the kitchen door. "I'll get it." I went to the door, snapping the thread.

"You are four years old!" Mom exclaimed in frustration.

I opened the door and our next-door neighbor Babette bustled inside. She was a large colorful woman with curly blond hair and a big heart, who, along with the rest of the town, adopted me and Mom years ago. "Oh, hiya, baby doll."

"Hi, Babette."

"You want some coffee?" Mom offered.

"Oh, no thanks, I just came over to ask a great big favor."

"Ask away," Mom said as she went to get some coffee for Babette anyway.

"Well, see, Morey just got a call to play a gig at the Village Vanguard tonight, so we gotta go to New York." Morey, Babette's husband, is a jazz pianist. I love the summers when all the windows are open and we can hear Morey playing. He's always dressed in black and is at least one foot taller than Babette, so watching them walk down the street is an odd sight.

"Oh, wow!" Mom said as she handed Babette her mug. "Cream?"

"And sugar. Thanks. Anyway, yesterday Morey and I finally broke down and got a new baby, you know?"

That could only mean one thing for Morey and Babette. A kitten. "What's its name?"

"Apricot!" Babette gushed. "Oh, he's the cutest thing, but he's so teeny. There's no way he can go with us, and I'd hate for him to stay all alone in the house. So I was thinking that maybe Rory could come over and house-sit for the evening."

"I'd love to."

"Oh, great!" Babette exclaimed. "We've got a kitchen full of food, and Morey just got cable so you can watch those four girls talking dirty if you want to."

I smiled. "Sounds good."

"You are an angel. Both of you. Angels. You have a key, right?"

"Yep," Mom said. "We got it covered."

"Ah! Great. All right, I'll leave you the number of where we're staying. Have a good time. We'll be back tomorrow morning. I love you crazy girls. Bye!"

The door slammed behind her.

"Wow," Mom said. "I can't believe how fast you jumped at a chance to spend the night away from me."

I started gathering my stuff for school and put it in my backpack. "You're crazy. I'm doing her a favor."

"Um hmm. Um hmm. *Sure* you are."

"Mom —"

"No, no, it's okay." She sighed dramatically. "Don't you worry about me. I'll be just fine."

"I'd like to debate you on that last subject, but I'm late for the bus."

"You know this is only like the second night we've ever spent apart. Doesn't that make you sad?"

"Yeah," I assured her. "I'll get over it."

"Uh huh. Well, Paul and Linda McCartney only spent eleven nights apart their entire relationship," she said, following me around the kitchen. "Did you know that?"

"I did not know that."

"Well, they were truly devoted to each other. Just being apart was too painful even to talk about."

"I understand."

"I don't think Linda would've even considered cat-sitting without Paul."

I stopped packing my bag for a second and looked at her. "You know, Mom. When I go off to college, I'm going to be gone every night. What will you do then?"

"Well, I . . . will go with you. I will sleep on the floor in your dorm next to your bed."

"Well, at least you got a plan." I grabbed my back-pack and headed out.

"Yes. Well, perhaps you'd like to take a picture of me with you tonight," she said, following me down the hall to the front door, "you know, in case you get lonely, you can talk to it . . . ?"

"Bye," I said as I headed out the door.

∽

I glanced up from my book as the bus that brings me home from Chilton came into town. As it pulled up to the bus stop, I saw Dean sitting on the back of the bus stop bench. A pleasant surprise. He stared at the bird-cage I was carrying as I got off the bus. "Carry your bird, miss?" he asked.

"Hi," I said. "I didn't expect to see you here."

"I just wanted to say hello," he said.

He leaned down and gave me a kiss.

I smiled. "Hello."

"Hello." He leaned in to kiss me again.

"Hello," I repeated.

Dean grabbed the birdcage and we started walking, passing our resident town troubadour, Grant, who was singing on the corner with his guitar.

"So, who's your friend?" Dean asked, motioning to the cage.

"Homework."

"Really."

"We will be cohabitating for the next month so I can examine its every move. Jealous?"

He laughed. "I'll get over it."

"So, hey. I'm house-sitting tonight for Babette, and I was thinking, maybe, if the right offer came along, I might be up to some company."

"Well, I'm offering."

"I'm accepting."

"Good."

I smiled. The world seemed perfect—I'd done well on my history test and the sun was shining. "Do you want to get some coffee?" I asked.

Dean sighed. "I can't, I have to get to work."

"I thought you worked at five o'clock."

He shook his head. "Nope, four on Thursdays. For some reasons, Thursdays are really busy." He chuckled. "Lots of oppressed housewives shopping for their husbands' dinners."

Bam.

I stopped walking. "Wow."

Dean stopped and turned around. "What?"

"That was a little pointed."

Dean looked totally confused. "What are you talking about?"

I stared at him, even more amazed that he didn't realize what he'd said. "That crack about the housewives shopping for their husbands' dinners."

Dean laughed. "Come on, it was a joke."

"Yeah, well, it was a pretty weird joke to hear coming out of your mouth."

Finally he realized I was serious and he frowned. "You are so sensitive about that whole Donna Reed thing."

"I am not sensitive about it!" I replied hotly. "I just find it ridiculous."

"Why?"

"What do you mean, why?"

He shrugged. "So she cooked a lot."

"A *lot*?" I exclaimed. "She made homemade doughnuts, chocolate cake, a lamb chops/mashed potato dinner, and enough stew to feed Cambodia all in one episode."

"So what?"

"You really like that concept, don't you?" I snapped.

"No . . . I," he protested. "Well, yeah. Sort of."

"Oh my God." I started walking again and Dean followed.

"I mean, it's a little over the top," Dean went on, "but the general idea of a wife cooking dinner for her husband and family, that's nice." He studied my expression. "Why is that not nice?"

"It's not just that," I insisted. "It's the having to have the dinner on the table as soon as the husband gets home, and having to look perfect to do housework, and the whole concept that her one point in life is to serve somebody else."

"Fine. Yes," he said, beginning to sound as angry as I felt. "But maybe there are two points of view here."

I folded my arms. "I don't think so."

"Well, you just feel that way because your mother feels that way!"

"Oh, what, so I have no opinions of my own."

"I didn't mean that!"

"Well, if I have no opinions of my own, then I guess I'd be just the kind of girl you like."

A few people walked by, staring with interest at our heated discussion. Dean pulled me aside and lowered his voice. "Rory, my mom used to make dinner for my dad every night before she started working, and now she does it on the weekends. What does that say about her?"

"It says that she has the choice and Donna Reed didn't."

"You do realize that Donna Reed wasn't real, don't you?"

"Yes, I know she wasn't real. But she represented millions of women who were real and who had to dress like that and act like that and—"

"Okay, can you please tell me how we got into an argument about *The Donna Reed Show*?"

"I don't know!"

We both stood there, frustrated. Our first real argument.

At last Dean sighed. "Okay, look. I gotta go to work, so . . . bye."

He turned and headed toward Doose's Market without looking back.

"Dean," I called after him.

"What?" He half turned.

I held out my hand. "Bird?"

He looked at me in confusion, then glanced down at the birdcage he was carrying. "Oh."

He handed me the bird.

I took it.

We parted without another word and I headed home.

3

When I got home, Mom was at the dining room table, cutting up decorating and home magazines. "Hey, good, I'm just about to leave," she called to me.

I dumped my book bag on the living room floor. "Where're you going?"

"To Luke's. We're picking out paint colors tonight. It's going to be hours of *Yes! No! Yes! No! Yes! No!* until my world-famous perseverance wears him down and he winds up in a ball on the floor crying like a girl. Wanna come watch?"

"I'm house-sitting tonight, remember?"

"Yes, but you gotta eat. Come have a quick burger."

"No, thanks." I went into the dining room and set the cage down on the table.

Mom immediately melted into a pile of goo. She loves baby anythings. "What is *that*?"

"It's for school." I propped open the small cage door and filled the food cup from a plastic bag of birdseed.

"Awww, he's so cute," Mom cooed. "What's his name?

"Case Study Number 12."

"Is that hyphenated?" Mom frowned at me. "Honey, he's adorable. He should have a name."

"I am not bonding with my midterm, thank you."

"All right, *I'll* name it." Mom peered into the cage and spoke to the chick in a baby-talk voice. "Hi. Your name is Stanley. Hi, Stanley."

"It's a girl." I brushed birdseed off my hands and went into my room.

"Oh. Sorry about the Stanley thing." She thought a moment. "Your name is *Stella*!" she told the chick. "Stella's nice—hey, and Stella was married to Stanley!" she hollered at me.

"Call it whatever you want."

"Man, are you grumpy," Mom said. "What happened?"

"Nothing. Just a long day."

"You know what the remedy for a long day is?" Mom said. "A ringside seat while Luke envisions strangling me with his baseball cap."

I loaded up my backpack with things to study, toothbrush, and a change of clothes, then I headed back into the dining room. "I'm gonna leave the chick here for the night so the kitten doesn't get any fancy ideas."

"Okay."

"She's already fed, and if she gets too loud, just put her in my room. I'll call you later."

I grabbed my coat off the table and turned to go, but Mom called me back.

"Hey . . . are you okay?" she asked softly.

I know I can tell my mom anything but somehow I didn't feel like talking about it. What could I say, anyway? That Dean and I had argued about Donna Reed?

"Yeah, just a bad afternoon," I told her. "I'll fix it."

"Okay. Call me if you need a wrench or something."

I smiled. "I will."

✎

Over at Babette's house, I followed her detailed instructions for Apricot, measuring out the food, adding some tuna fish and giving the mixture a whirl with a hand mixer. I took it off the counter and placed it on a crocheted place mat where the tiny little tabby, Apricot, patiently waited for his dinner. I'm a little surprised he didn't hop up on the counter to get the food himself; the distance isn't that far. This was the diminutive Babette's house before she married Morey. Everything is downsized to accommodate her short stature: the tabletops, the counters, the kitchen sink, etc. When they married, everything stayed the same and Morey adjusted. Every time Morey walks through a doorway, he ducks but never loses stride.

I sat down on the couch, where I'd spread out all my schoolwork, and tried to study, but the words ran together on the page. I wondered what Mom was doing. Maybe I should call her and talk about this Dean thing. Maybe it would help . . . But then I remembered. She'd be over at Luke's by now, talking about paint.

Of course, there was one other person I could talk to about it. I closed my book and went into the kitchen for the cordless phone. I punched in the familiar numbers and moved back to the couch to sit down.

"Hi. Is Dean in? This is Rory . . . Oh. Well, would you tell him I called? Okay, thanks."

I hung up and laid the phone on the coffee table. As I stared at the phone, a vague idea began to take shape in my mind.

I grabbed my coat and dashed out the door.

∽

Soon I was at Lane's house—my best friend outside of my mom. I hurried up the stairs to her room and tapped on the door. "Lane?"

"Yo!" she called out.

I opened her door and found her studying at her desk. "Hey, how's it going?"

"Very well," she said. "I have discovered that in addition to my lameness in geometry, I will also not become a biologist, French translator, or Civil War buff."

"So that just leaves bass player in the Foo Fighters."

"I also wouldn't rule out keyboardist in the Siouxsie and the Banshees reunion tour."

"I like that you keep an open mind."

"So, what's up?"

"I need to borrow a CD."

"Which one?"

"The weird one."

"Need more information."

"Well, it has this . . . instrument in it."

"As opposed to all those instrumentless CDs that are so popular with the kids nowadays?"

"I don't remember what it is, but I'll know it when I see it."

She shoved back from her desk. "Okay. Let's have a

look." She hurried over to her window seat, dropped to her knees.

Lane lives for music. Her vast CD collection rivals that of many indie music stores. But her traditional and conservative Korean-born parents disapprove, so Lane's collection must be somewhat . . . underground. Yes, I mean hidden beneath the floor of her room.

Lane slid back one of the polished wide-plank floorboards. Dozens of CDs were lined up in alphabetical order.

"Okay," she said, pointing to each section, "so we have Classic Rock, Progressive Rock, Pretty Boy Rock . . ."

"Excuse me?"

"Bon Jovi, Duran Duran, the Wallflowers, Bush . . ."

I nodded. "Got it." But it was not what I was looking for. "Next."

She slid the board back into place, crawled across her bed, then lifted another floorboard on the other side. "Punk, New Wave, German Metal bands, Broadway, Soundtracks . . ."

"Interesting filing system," I said.

"Anything yet?"

"No. Sorry."

She replaced the board and thought a moment. "Okay, well, over there we have Jazz, Jazz Vocals, Classical, Country, Rock-a-Billy, Sinatra, the Capitol Years . . ." Then she clapped her hands. "Oh, wait. The Miscellaneous section."

"Hey, that sounds good."

I followed her to the other side of the room, just in front of her dresser.

As she slid back the floorboard, I could tell this was one of her favorite sections.

"William Shatner!" I said, impressed, as I picked up one of the CDs. "Is this the one where he sings 'Tambourine Man'?"

"And 'Lucy in the Sky With Diamonds,'" she exclaimed proudly.

"Hey, remind me to get this for my mom for her birthday." I slipped it back into place. "Oh, wait!" I pulled out a CD and checked the cover. "Hey! That's it!" I studied the playlist on the back of the plastic case. *Perfect.* "Can I?"

Lane shrugged. "Take it."

"Thanks!" I grabbed my jacket and headed out. I was starting to get excited.

"So, what are you doing?" Lane asked as she replaced the floorboard.

"Um, I'm not completely sure yet."

"Okay!" she shouted as I flew down the stairs. "But I want details!"

⁓

Soon, everything was ready. When the phone rang, I grabbed it. "Hello?"

"I wasn't sure if you still wanted me to come over." Dean.

"Oh, I do. I do! I *absolutely* do!"

"Are you sure?"

"I'm totally, completely—" I heard him laugh on the other end of the line. "You're teasing me."

"A little. But I did appreciate the enthusiasm."

"So, how long until you get here?"

"Actually, not long at all."

"Why? Where are you?"

"Right outside."

I hung up, ran to the door and opened it.

Dean was out on the sidewalk putting his cell phone into the pocket of his leather jacket.

He looked up and his jaw dropped. "What the . . ."

"Honey, you're home!" I sang out.

∽4

Dean just stared at me. Who could blame him?

I was wearing an orange sleeveless fifties dress, with tiny little buttons down the front and a huge skirt with layers of crinoline underneath filling it out. Topping it off? A pair of matching orange pointy-toed high heels. Donna Reed, come to life.

"Well, say something." I smiled sweetly and smoothed down my frilly apron.

"Uh, trick-or-treat?" Dean responded.

"What, you don't like it?" I twirled on my heels to give the full effect.

"Uh, no. I do!" he blurted out. "It's, uh . . ." He waved his hand in the air, searching for the right thing to say. "It's got a large circumference."

"Thank you. Now come on in. It's cold outside." I headed inside, ducking a little to avoid hitting Babette's shortened door frame.

Dean hesitantly climbed the steps and followed me in.

"Oh my God," he said once he was inside.

I glanced around Babette's house, pleased at what I'd accomplished in so short a time. A fire blazed in the fireplace and candles glowed all over the room including the dining room table, which was set with flowers and the good china—a romantic dinner for two. "Flower Girl of Bordeaux" by Juan Esquivel was playing on the stereo. "Here. Let me take your coat."

"Thank you."

"You're welcome." I pulled his jacket from his shoulders and hung it up on the hall tree. When I turned around, Dean was moving cautiously into the living room.

"Interesting music," Dean commented.

"I'm glad you like it." Esquivel has been dubbed the "King of Space Age Pop." If you ever have a chance to check out Esquivel's music and life, do it. He rightly belongs in Lane's "Miscellaneous" CD Section.

"So what's that?" He pointed to an oval tray of crackers with whipped cheese on them.

"Oh, just some appetizers before dinner."

"Before dinner?"

"Yes."

"Are we going out?"

"No." I held up the tray like a perfect little hostess and he stuffed one in his mouth.

"Ordering pizza?"

"Nope."

"Oh. So . . ."

"I made you dinner."

"Excuse me?"

"Steak, green beans, mashed potatoes . . ."

"You made me *dinner*?"

"That's right."

"*You* . . . made *me* . . . dinner."

"And dessert."

Dean looked totally confused. "Okay, what is going on here?"

"I'm sorry. I thought it was obvious." I smiled. "It's Donna Reed night."

I dragged Dean over to the table and placed him in his seat. I chose some dinner music, starting with Shelley Fabares's "Johnny Angel," and then I served him a home-cooked meal that would have made Donna Reed proud.

"Well?" I asked after he had a chance to sample the meal.

"What can I say?"

"You can say it's perfect."

"It's perfect."

"Thank you. Now, how is it really?"

"It's . . . *perfect*."

"Yeah?"

"It's amazing." He shook his head. "I mean, I've never had anybody make dinner for me before. Except my mom, and believe me, it's not the same."

We smiled at each other across the candlelight.

"I'm extremely glad to hear that."

Dean reached for another helping of mashed potatoes.

"Wait!" I said. "You want to save room for dessert, right?"

"Oh, right." He sat back. "So what's for dessert?"

I grinned. "Lime Fantasy Supreme."

"Which is?"

I jumped up and ran to the refrigerator, then turned around, holding up two parfait glasses. "Green Jell-O and Cool Whip."

Dean laughed out loud. "You are insane!"

But as I turned to put our dessert back, I spotted something. There, in the fridge, was the tube of dinner rolls. "Oh no. I forgot the rolls."

"What?"

I pulled out the tube and returned to the table to show Dean. "I was going to make rolls!"

"Well, that's okay."

"I can't believe I forgot them." Frowning, I started pounding the tube on the table, trying to make it pop open. But it just bounced on the table edge.

"What are you doing?" Dean exclaimed.

"I'll make them now." I whacked the tube again and again.

"Okay, whoa! Hold on. Come on—" Dean grabbed my hands and pulled me into his lap, then removed the tube and laid it on the table.

"We *really* don't need rolls," he said gently.

"Donna would've *never* forgotten the rolls," I said with a pout. "They're going to make me turn in my pearls."

Dean laughed and gave me a long, sweet kiss.

When we pulled apart, he grinned. "I promise I'll kick anyone's butt who comes near those pearls."

I smiled and he kissed me again. Then he sighed. "Rory . . ."

"Yeah?"

"As really amazing as this whole thing was, I mean,

the music, the outfit, the dinner . . . I hope you know that I don't expect you to be Donna Reed. I don't *want* you to be Donna Reed. That's not what I meant. This whole thing just got totally blown out of proportion. I'm actually pretty happy with you."

"I know," I said. "And I appreciate that. But aside from this actually being fun, I did a little research on Donna Reed."

"You did *research* on Donna Reed?"

"Look." I got up and grabbed the pages I'd printed out from the Internet. "See, she *did* do the whole milk-and-cookies, wholesome, big-skirt thing, but aside from that she was also an uncredited producer and director on her television show, which made her one of the first women television executives, which is actually pretty impressive."

"Well, I'm glad this turned out to be such a positive experience for you."

"It has been. And even though I probably will never get the feeling back in my left little toe," I added, "I would do it again."

"Yeah?"

"Someday." I smiled at Dean.

"But for now, I had better get these dishes cleaned up." I stood and began clearing the table.

Dean jumped to his feet. "I'll help."

"Sorry," I quipped. "You're a man. You can't help for another fifteen years."

"Okay, well, then," Dean said, "as the man, I will do what the man is supposed to do."

"Go bowling?"

"Take out the trash."

We laughed, glad that things were all right between us again.

Dean took out the trash and I hurried to clear the table, carrying the dishes to the kitchen. I reset the table and pulled our desserts out of the refrigerator, then set them in place. Dean hadn't come back in so I started loading the dishwasher.

A few minutes later, Dean still hadn't returned and our desserts were starting to look odd so I ran out on the back porch to look for him.

"Hey, the Jell-O is doing this weird melty thing and—"

I froze.

Dean was just standing there in the side yard, holding his bag of garbage, while Luke was standing on the other side of the yard, holding a box filled with trash, one of our lamps, now broken, sticking out of it.

Mom and I stood like mirror images, facing each other across the railings of the two houses' side porches.

"Oh, Mom. Luke."

"Rory," Luke greeted.

"Hi," I said nonchalantly, as if I weren't wearing a huge-skirted fifties dress, with my boyfriend standing in the yard taking out the trash.

"Ah . . . what the hell were you two doing?" Mom said bluntly.

"Nothing!" Dean said quickly. "She, uh, we ate dinner, you know, steak and then beans . . ."

"Canned," I pointed out.

Mom nodded. "Canned."

"Not fresh," I said.

"No," Luke said.

"No," Mom repeated.

"And potatoes," Dean explained, as if that would make things all right.

"From a box," I added.

"But they were still good." Dean turned and smiled at me.

"Thank you."

"You're welcome."

Mom and Luke just kept staring at us.

Then I wondered what Luke was doing over at our house at this time of night. "So what were *you* guys doing?" I asked innocently.

Luke went all weird at that and turned to Mom for an answer.

"Us? Oh, we were just . . . uh, in the house . . ."

"Yeah," Luke said, "and then the lamp sort of . . . I'm gonna get going."

"Yeah," Mom said.

"I'm sorry about the . . ." Luke continued.

"Oh. Forget it," Mom replied.

"Bye," he muttered and took off.

Dean turned and looked at me. "I'd probably better go too," he said. "Thanks for dinner."

"You're welcome."

And then it was just me and Mom staring at each other. I stood there with my arms crossed, waiting. And then Mom cocked her head at me and grinned.

I shifted uncomfortably. "What?" I said.

"Okay, so you're sixteen," Mom said. "You have a whole house to yourself for the evening, I *expect* you to have your boyfriend over." Then she started to giggle. "But what is with the apron?"

I shrugged. "It's a long story."

"Does it involve a sharp blow to the head?"

I just smiled and gestured over my shoulder. "I gotta go check on Apricot."

"Oh my God! I just saw the *pearls*!"

"I'm going in now," I announced. I pushed open the door.

"Yes. Good. I have to go in too," Mom said, on the verge of hysterical laughter. "I have to write down all the ways that I am going to torture you about that outfit."

"Good night!" I called out cheerfully.

"Oh, could I just get a picture, though?" Mom called after me. "'Cause visual aids would really help. Oh! Oh, the shoes!" she shrieked. "I'm dying!"

I rolled my eyes and shut the door.

Inside I glanced around the kitchen and living room, at the candles still glowing, the Supreme Lime Fantasy on the table. Remembering how nice it all was . . .

I turned to check on Apricot.

I'd left her sleeping on an embroidered cushion on the couch. But now she was gone.

I called her name as I quickly searched the house.

Did I leave the door open when I went outside?

Panicking, I ran out the door. "Mom!" I shouted. "I can't find Apricot!"

"What? *No!*"

"He was on the couch when I came out and now he's nowhere!"

"Okay. That is it. We are not animal people! Period!" And she rushed over to help me find the kitten. We finally found him curled up in one of Morey's slippers. Then I got Mom to tell me why Luke was at our house. She admitted Stella had gotten loose from her cage and she had called Luke to help her.

I wondered why, of all the people in town, she had called Luke. She said it was because she had just spent the evening with him but sometimes I wonder about those two.

But before I could ask Mom more, she saw the green Jell-O and Cool Whip and I was forced to shove her out the door to get some peace.

∾5

The next night we showed up at Grandma and Grandpa's house for our regular Friday night dinner. We rang the bell, and waited. Rang again. Knocked. No one came. That was enough for Mom to turn around and go home, but I wouldn't let her. We were already there; and I knew there was no way Grandma and Grandpa would stand us up.

While we continued to wait for the door to open, Mom started in again on the Donna Reed outfit. All the way over here, same topic, with slight variations. This time she suggested we both dress up whenever we watch *The Donna Reed Show* — get kind of a twisted *Rocky Horror Picture Show* thing going.

I desperately knocked again, hoping the door would open. Miraculously, it finally did.

"Lorelai, Rory," Grandma said in a rush.

"Hey, I thought maybe the doorbell was out, 'cause—" Mom started to say.

"Come in, come in!"

"—we were out here ringing the bell for a while and—" Mom continued.

But Grandma had already rushed away.

Mom and I exchanged a look.

"Okay," she said to me. "Guess we should go in now."

We headed for the living room where we heard my grandparents speaking with another man on the speaker-phone. We entered, and discovered Grandma and Grandpa pacing around the room.

"And that would be the same as what we were paying for our old place?" Grandma said.

"Exactly the same," said the man on the phone.

"Except for the grounds fee," Grandpa stated.

"Well, the grounds fee is higher," agreed phone man.

Mom and I looked at each other, wondering what we stepped into. We took off our jackets as they continued.

"But the grounds are larger, Richard," Grandma said.

"I'm just trying to get all the information, Emily," he responded.

"All the information is that this is our last chance to go to Martha's Vineyard for the season. That's all the information," Grandma replied.

"I realize the position we are in, but this is a business transaction," Grandpa stated.

"Oh, for heaven's sake," Grandma said.

Mom opened her purse and pulled out a half-eaten pack of gummy bears as we settled in to watch the show and Grandma and Grandpa did not disappoint.

"As a business transaction, one in which money goes

out and we receive certain goods and services . . . ,"
Grandpa continued.

"And he's patronizing me. How lovely."

". . . I must treat this conversation with the same care
and devotion to detail I would any other conversation
that would be considered a business transaction. Kindly
allow me to do so."

"Richard! Emily! Please!" the man shouted over the
speakerphone.

"Goodness, you startled me," Grandma said.

"I'm sorry. I just wanted to say that I'm sure we
could negotiate the grounds fee."

"Well, I'm sure that would be fine," Grandpa said.
They wrapped up the conversation and hung up the
phone, looking quite pleased.

"What's going on," Mom asked.

"Oh, your mother and I just secured a place in
Martha's Vineyard," Grandpa said smugly.

"Really?" I said. "That's great."

"I thought you lost your old place," Mom said.

"We did," Grandma said. "But this afternoon we
found out that Arthur Roundtree has died."

"He'd been drinking," Grandpa revealed.

"So we got on the phone"—Grandma snapped her
fingers—"and snatched that place up!"

I looked at my mom. She was as stunned as I was.

"Fine piece of property," Grandpa was saying.

"Much better than our usual place," Grandma agreed.
They looked thrilled.

"The both of you are going directly to hell," Mom
said. "I hope you know that."

"Well, at least we'll be well rested." Grandpa chor-
tled at his little joke.

"Touché," Mom replied.

"The two of you must come up for a weekend," Grandma gushed. "It is so lovely. Rory would just love it."

"Can we go for a weekend?" I asked Mom.

She patted my hand. "We'll see how much Valium Aunt Sookie can loan Mommy, okay?"

"The only drawback is that, of course, we had to rent the place furnished," Grandma went on, "and Arthur had dreadful taste. Remember the library, Richard?" She reached for his hand.

Grandpa patted her hand in his and laughed heartily. "Green and pink! Horrible, just horrible."

"Well, he's dead now, so I guess he got his," Mom added.

My grandparents froze and stared at her, mortified.

"Lorelai!" Grandma scolded. "You're being morbid."

Mom's mouth fell open. "*I'm* being morbid?"

"New subject, please," I piped up.

"Joan and Melissa Rivers here are telling me *I'm* being morbid!" Mom muttered.

I elbowed her.

"Rory," Grandma said, reaching for her drink and smiling, as if the previous conversation had never happened, "what's new in your life?"

I shrugged. "Not much. Just school, homework . . ."

"Aprons," Mom said.

I glared at her. "Do not go there."

But of course, Grandma hears all things you don't want her to hear. "What did you mean, aprons?"

"Nothing, Mom. I was just teasing her."

"I don't understand."

"It's not important," Mom said.

"Then humor me," Grandma insisted.

"It's nothing. Rory got dressed up in a cute apron the other day and I was just teasing her about it."

"Why did you get dressed up in an apron?" Grandpa asks.

Mom looked at me.

I gave her the slightest shake of my head. No. Please.

"Well," Mom said, "we've decided to give up that pesky Harvard dream and focus on something more realistic. Mom . . . Dad . . ." She laid a hand on my shoulder and smiled, as if it were the proudest day of her life. "Rory's decided to become a maid, just like I was."

The world stopped spinning for a second as my grandparents stared at us.

"Is that funny?" Grandma finally choked out. She turned toward Grandpa. "Did she think that was funny?"

Grandpa was equally stunned. "What would possess you to say such a thing?"

"And in front of Rory!" Grandma added.

"I was kidding," Mom said. I think she was a little amused by the rise she was getting out of them.

"God!" Grandma's hand went to her chest. "My heart stopped."

Grandpa reached for his glass of Scotch.

"Why don't you tell them about your bird?" Mom suggested, patting me on the leg. "That seems like a safe subject."

"Your bird?" Grandpa took a drink.

I nodded in relief. "Yeah, it's for school. Each of us has to follow a chick through its entire growth process. Everything has to be logged. Eating habits. Sleeping habits—"

"Houdini habits," Mom interjected.

"She got out," I explained.

"And she ran far."

"But she lived."

"And she's a better bird for it."

"Thank God Luke found her," I said.

"*Luke* found her?" Grandma immediately asked.

Mom grimaced. "What?"

"Rory said that Luke found her."

"Getting back at me for the apron thing, huh?" Mom muttered.

"Sorry," I whispered back.

"Did the bird get loose in Luke's Diner?" Grandma pressed.

Mom shook her head. "The bird got loose at home."

"Your home," Grandma clarified.

"Ye-es." Mom jumped up and headed for the bar.

"Ah."

I quickly tried to change the subject. "So, Grandpa, when is your next trip?"

"Madrid on the twelfth."

"Wow."

"I believe there may be a nice copy of Cervantes in it for you," he said with a smile. Great literature is one thing we have in common, and he supports my habit by regularly contributing to my library of prized hardcovers.

"*Gracias*," I replied.

I glanced at Grandma. It wasn't working. It seemed the only word she'd heard in the past ten minutes was "Luke."

"What was Luke doing at your house?" she asked Mom.

Mom tensed. "Oh, look. No ice," she said, holding up the ice bucket. "I'll get some." And she escaped to the kitchen.

Grandma was instantly on her heels. "I asked you a question."

They were talking so loud I could hear every word.

"He was helping me find the bird, Mom."

"Really?"

"Yes, really."

"And how did he know that the bird was missing? What, was he strolling by the house when he heard your plaintive cries for help?"

"Mom . . ."

"Or the helpless cheeps of a chick in trouble?"

"I called him, Mom. Okay? I called him and asked him to come over and help me find the bird. Okay?"

"It seems like this man is always around when you're in trouble."

"He is a good friend."

"Oh, please." "Do we have to discuss this?" Mom asked, desperate to end the conversation.

"Lorelai, I'm getting a little tired of being lied to."

"Apparently we do."

"This man was at Rory's birthday party. He came with you to the hospital. He's the male lead in every story you tell. You go to his diner every day. I've seen the way he looks at you, the way you look at him. I am not a fool."

"Mom, pleeeeease."

"Why do you treat me like I don't have a clue in the world as to what is going on in your life?" There was a hurt sound in her voice. "Now, I am asking you, as a favor, if you have any respect for me at all as your mother, just tell me—do you have feelings for this man?"

"I don't know. Maybe I do. I haven't given it that much thought . . . maybe I do."

"Thank you," Grandma said quietly. "I'm glad you

were finally honest with me." Then: "Now we can discuss what on earth you could possibly be thinking!"

Mom and Grandma eventually returned to the living room and we continued on with dinner as if we had never gotten into the discussion about aprons, kittens, chicks and Luke.

∽

The next afternoon, on my way home from the library, I spotted Mom and Luke. They had just finished unloading cans and cans and cans of paint from the back of his truck to the front of the diner. Mom headed off, so I ran to catch up with her. "Hey!"

"Hey, you," she said as she draped her arm around me and we headed down the sidewalk together. She was in a great mood. The streets were wet from a passing rain, but the sun was out, leaving tree branch shadows on the sidewalk.

"Jeeze, you think he got enough paint?" I asked.

"I know." Mom nodded. "I tried to tell him. So, dinner. Thoughts?"

"Let's have some," I said firmly.

"How about Chinese?"

"Sounds good."

"Great. I need to stop at the market and get some fruit," she said.

"Why?"

"I think I'm getting scurvy."

"Really."

"Yeah. Well, that or a cold. But either way, I need fruit."

We arrived at Doose's Market, where huge bins just

outside the door were filled with oranges, apples, pears, and grapes.

We were picking out fruit when suddenly a motorcycle roared around the square.

Taylor Doose came out of his market to glare. "Damn motorcycles! They're a *scourge*."

"Yeah!" I said, in mock outrage.

"Yeah!" Mom joined in.

"They're loud, they're dangerous. We should ban them from town," Taylor declared.

"Hmm. Maybe we should set up barricades and ban all unwelcome strangers from crossing the border," Mom said.

Taylor shoved his hands in the pockets of his slacks and nodded—totally unaware that Mom was mocking him—then he realized . . .

"Well . . . well, no, we couldn't do that. That would be illegal."

"Darn laws," Mom said.

The biker gunned his motor.

"Ah! I've got to get away from this noise!" And Taylor scurried back into the market.

Mom slipped her arm through mine and walked toward the street to get a better look. "Kill me and bury me with that bike," she said dreamily.

"What is it, a Harley?" I asked.

"*That* is a 2000 Indian, eighty-horsepower, five-speed close ratio Andrews transmission. And I want to get one."

"No," I said firmly.

"Why not?"

"You'd die."

"Oh. That."

And then said bike pulled up to the curb, cut the lights, then the motor. We turned and headed back into the market.

"Hey!" the rider called out.

We couldn't see his face—he was wearing a shiny black helmet and dark sunglasses—but I knew I hadn't seen that motorcycle around town before.

Mom stopped and glanced warily over her shoulder. She stared at the biker. Then she said, "Hi."

I was halfway in the market already, but I stopped and peeked back out when I heard the biker say, "Nice shirt. . . ." He got off the bike. "Take it off." We were stunned. Who did this guy think he was?

Together we watched as the biker pulled off his helmet.

"*Christopher* . . ." Mom whispered.

"*Dad!*" I screamed, flying into his arms.

~6

My dad grabbed me and swung me around.

"This is great!" I shouted when he set me down. "What are you doing here?"

"I'm here to see you...and your mom"—He glanced sideways at her—"who's not saying anything about as loud as a person can."

"Hello," Mom said, still stunned.

"A word!" Dad exclaimed. "Huh! Perhaps there's a phrase in my future." But then he glanced past her and lowered his voice. "Okay, why is that man staring at me?"

Mom followed his gaze as I answered, "Oh, that's Taylor Doose. He owns the market. He knows all and sees all!"

"So, um! What's with the just showing up, Mr. Spontaneity Guy?" Mom asked.

Dad shrugged. "Well, my folks are back in Connecticut, so I'm here to see them, and on the way I thought I'd stop by and surprise the Gilmore girls. Are you surprised?"

"Oh. The teeniest feather could . . . knock me in the gutter," Mom said.

"So where would somebody find someplace to stay around here?" he asks me.

"Stay? Really? You're staying?" This was too good to be true.

"I'm thinking about it."

"Stay with us!" I said, getting more and more excited.

Mom squirmed. "Um . . . sweetie . . ."

Dad was a little uncomfortable too. "I don't think your mom wants to—"

"No, no, no, it's not that," Mom insisted, "it's just that . . . I'm still surprised."

"Mom, *please*!" I begged.

Mom sighed and gave in. "Why don't you stay with us for a couple days?" she said to him.

Dad beamed. "Thanks, Lor! You won't even know I'm there." Then he turned to me and pointed at his bike. "Hey! Hop on!"

"Hop *off*," Mom said instantly.

I stopped and turned back to her.

"Hop on." Dad handed me the helmet.

"Hop off."

"Lorelai . . ." Dad gave her one of his most charming smiles. I added one of my own.

Mom sighed and surrendered. "Hop on."

I pulled on the helmet, climbed on behind Dad, and we roared away. I glanced back for the tiniest second and caught Mom standing there, shaking her head.

∽

When we got home, Dad went upstairs to shower while I fixed up a bed for him on the couch in the living room.

I piled on tons of blankets, wanting to make it as cozy and comfortable as possible.

"He looks good, don't you think?" I asked Mom, who was pacing.

"He looks good," she agreed.

"I like his hair shorter."

"Shorter's nice."

"Do you think he'll stay here long?" I asked without looking at her.

"I wouldn't bet a lot of money on it," she said softly.

"Maybe we can get him to stay for a couple of weeks," I said, tucking in another blanket.

"Absolutely," she said. "By weighting him down with blankets."

Okay, so maybe I was going a little overboard. But I was so excited. "I just want him to be comfortable."

"He's going to come and go as he pleases, babe," she said in a low, serious voice. "You know that."

"Yeah. I know," I admitted.

"And no amount of bedding is going to change that."

"Yeah, but he's never come to Stars Hollow before," I pointed out.

"I know."

"Well, that means something's gotta be different, right?" I looked at her.

Mom smiled wistfully. "Why don't you just enjoy the time you've got, okay?"

I stopped piling blankets for a second and turned to my mom.

"Yeah, okay." I smiled and turned back to fluffing pillows that were already fluffed. I understood why Mom was wary. But I also knew *she* was the one who chose to give him up, not the other way around.

"I still think something's different, though," I said.

Mom looked like she was about to say something else, but then Dad came down the stairs, his hair wet, a towel slung around his neck.

"That is the worst shower I have ever had!" he complained with a grin as he came into the living room. "The water pressure keeps changing every two seconds. I am fixing it tomorrow."

"Hey, you stay away from my shower," Mom warned.

I smiled, watching them.

"We ordered Chinese food," I told Dad. "It should be here any minute."

"Good. I'm starving."

"Here." Mom handed him a mug of coffee.

"Hey, how's Diane?" I said, hugging a crocheted afghan to my chest.

Dad looked a little uncomfortable. "Uh, Diane is ancient history," he said with a lopsided grin.

That didn't seem to surprise Mom too much as she sat down on the couch.

"When I met her at Easter, you said she could be the one," I said, a little surprised by the news.

"The one to be gone by Memorial Day," Dad joked as he joined Mom on the couch.

I made a face at him. "You're worse than Mom."

"Low blow!"

"Can't keep a feller happy?" Dad teased.

"Oh, I keep them happy," she responded. "I keep them *very* happy."

"Okay, now don't get gross!" I said.

"Yeah, you're upsetting us!" Dad added.

Actually, my mom was right. She could keep a guy happy. In fact, she recently broke up with my English teacher Max Medina because they were so happy they couldn't control themselves and started kissing like teenagers at Chilton's Parents' Night. And as luck would have it, Paris Geller, the classmate who would most like to see me fail, saw the whole thing and within minutes the news was all over the school. Grandma had even heard by our next Friday dinner. Mom said they broke up to protect me, but I think that's crap. But I do know their little incident nearly cost Mr. Medina his job, so until they learn to control themselves, maybe it's better that they're apart. It didn't really matter now, though. I was just really excited to have my dad around for a few days, and who knows? Maybe if they spent a little more time together, things would be different between them. Couldn't hurt to give them some time together.

"I'm going to study a little before the food gets here," I said innocently.

Dad stared at me in amazement. "What?"

"I like to get my weekend homework done and out of the way by Saturday night so then I can do extra credit stuff on Sunday," I explained.

As I headed to my room, I heard Mom mutter, "Don't look at me . . ."

I could hear them talking in the other room as I got my books out. It sounded really nice. Sometimes I used to lie awake at night, wondering what it would be like to fall asleep to the sound of my parents' voices talking low in the other room.

As I started my homework, I remembered I had plans the next morning and wondered if my dad would want to come. I hurried back into the living room. "Hey, I forgot to ask you, tomorrow morning I'm going to a softball game. Want to come?"

Dad was surprised. "You play softball?"

Mom and I laughed.

"Uh, no."

"Okay, fine," Dad said. "So whose game is it?"

"My friend Dean's."

"Dean?"

"Yeah, Dean. It starts at nine."

"Uh, sure. It's a date," he said.

I headed back to my room. I grinned when I heard Dad say, "She's got a Dean?"

"She's got a Dean," Mom confirmed.

The next morning Dad and I walked over to the ball field where a handful of townsfolk have a semiregular game with a semiregular group of spectators.

"So which is your Dean?" Dad asked as we headed toward the bleachers.

I pointed. "That's him over there." I pointed again. "And that's Luke."

"Luke's the diner guy."

"Yes. We eat there practically every day," I said as we sat down.

"Looks like we got out number three coming to the plate, guys!" Luke shouted to his teammates from the pitcher's mound as Dean stepped up to the plate.

"I'd send your boys a little farther back in the field, Luke," Dean replied.

"Why, will they have a better view of you whiffing?"

Dean laughed. "The only way I'm not hittin' it is if you don't have the strength to get it over the plate."

Kirk, one of the locals sitting behind us, piped up. "The truth of the matter is that you can't pitch and you can't hit. So this'll be a terrific match-up."

"Knock it off, Kirk," Luke called out.

"An historic lack of action!" Kirk continued.

"Don't you have better things to do with your weekends?" Luke asks.

"What can I say, I'm addicted to comedy," Kirk replied.

Dean noticed me then and gave me a quick wave as Kirk turned to me and my dad. "Half an hour they've been playing, and it's tied zero-zero." He focused back on the field and continued to heckle the players. "Hey, if you ever take this act on the road, I've got a name for you! Zero and Zero. Dean Zero and Luke Zero. Get it?"

"That doesn't even resemble clever!" Luke shouted back.

"I'm dumbing it down for you, Alfalfa."

Dad seemed as amused by this exchange as I was. "How long do these games last?"

" 'Til they get tired," I told him. "Then they just say 'the first team to get a run wins.' "

"Yeah, it's really professional down there," Kirk interjected. "Hey, Luke, does your husband play softball, too?"

"That's it!" Luke slammed his glove to the ground and headed toward the bleachers. Kirk quickly stood up. "I'm getting paged, I've gotta go!" he said as he hurried off.

Dean took advantage of the unexpected break and came over as my dad watched Kirk run off, thoroughly enjoying the show he just witnessed.

"Hey."

"Hey."

My dad and I stood up and I introduced them. "Dean, this is my dad. Dad, this is Dean."

Dad nodded. "Dean."

"Nice to meet you," Dean said politely.

"Same here."

"So, do you live in the area?" Dean asked.

"No, I had some time, so I rode my bike out from Berkeley."

Dean's eyes lit up. "Really. What do you got?"

"It's a 2000 Indian."

"I've got an '86 Suzuki."

"Nice."

"Yeah."

"Dean, come on!" Luke interrupted, now back on the mound.

"I gotta go," Dean said. "I'll see you later. It was nice meeting you."

Dad and I sat back down on the bench. He had this weird grin on his face. "So that was a Dean."

"That was a Dean," I said proudly.

Dean, now back on the field, turned to Luke. "Hey, next run wins, all right?" Luke looked at him and finally responded.

"Yeah. All right."

❧

After the game I gave Dad the VIP tour of Stars Hollow. "This is the town flower shop. Over there's the good pizza place, that's the stationery store, and that's Al's Pancake World."

"Good pancakes?"

"Oh, he doesn't serve pancakes."

"Okay."

"He switched to international cuisine a couple years ago and dropped the pancakes. He would've changed the name, but he had already printed about a million napkins with his original name, so he just kept it."

I could tell Dad was trying not to laugh. "What kind of international cuisine?"

"He kind of hops around. Last month was his salute to Paraguay."

"Anyone salute back?"

"Not really."

Then I heard someone calling out my name. "Rory, honey, how *are* you, sweetie?" I smiled as I turned around to greet Miss Patty, once a dancer on Broadway, but now owner and teacher at Stars Hollow's only dance studio. She can usually be counted on not only to know everything going on in town, but to help spread the word as well.

Today she had a glittery red shawl draped around her shoulders, her face made up as if she were ready to go out on the town.

"Miss Patty, this is my dad, Christopher."

Her eyes widened in sudden interest. "Your *dad*?"

"Nice to meet you." Dad shook Miss Patty's hand.

"You're Rory's father, well, well, well." She sized him up, then batted her eyes at him. "You know, Christopher, we're all like Rory's parents around here. I'm one of her mothers. And since you're her father, well, that would make us—a couple. A couple of what, I don't know!"

"Okay, well, we've got to go now," I said.

Miss Patty winked at Dad. "Come back and see me."

"I will," he assured her.

As we walked away, I glanced back over my shoulder and saw Miss Patty dialing her cell phone.

A second later we heard, "Well, you must be Rory's father!"

Taylor Doose had run up to greet us in the street. "Taylor Doose," he introduced himself. "Grocer to Stars Hollow."

Dad shook Taylor's hand. "It's very nice to meet you."

Dad slipped his arm around me as we headed off. "News travels fast here," he whispered.

"Yes, it does."

When we passed Stars Hollow Bookstore, Dad's eyes lit up and he pulled me toward the door. "Bookstore! Good. Come on." We entered through the glass door.

"Hey, hey, Christopher!" someone shouted.

It gave Dad a start as he turned to the voice.

A bearded man leaned back on the checkout counter, grinning broadly at Dad. He was dressed in a plaid orange lumberjack jacket, a sweater over blue-jean overalls, with a knit cap on his head. "Jackson Belleville!" he bellowed, introducing himself. He shook Dad's hand like they were old college buddies.

"Uh, hello," Dad said uncertainly.

Jackson smiled and leaned back on the counter. "Boy, I gotta tell you, did they get your description wrong."

Dad looked amused. "Really."

"Oh yeah. Much more George Clooney than Brad Pitt. Hey, Andrew," he said to the man behind the counter, who was also blatantly staring at my dad.

"Yeah?"

"Don't you think he's much more George Clooney than Brad Pitt?"

Andrew, owner of the bookstore, peered at Dad and shook his head. "I'm going with the Billy Crudup comparison myself."

"Really?"

"Oh yeah."

Jackson shook his head. "I don't see it. Maybe from the side. Hey, do you mind?" He reached up and grabbed my dad by the shoulders.

"What? Oh no. Not at all."

Jackson turned Dad from side to side, studying his profile. Dad was taking it all in stride.

"Ah, well, eh, there's a little Crudup in there," Jackson finally admitted. "Huh. We-e-e-ll, it's nice to meetcha, whoever you look like."

"Nice to meet you too," Dad replied. He grinned at me as he pulled me away from the front counter and we walked around the store. "Okay, I'm kidnapping you and getting you out of here," he said under his breath.

"They all mean well."

"Yes, I'm sure all lunatics have the best intentions." He smiled. "Okay, so I hear you like books."

"Why, yes, I do."

"Well, I would like you to pick something out and let me buy it for you," Dad said, motioning to the shelves.

"Dad! You don't have to buy me anything."

"Come on," he insisted. "What's the book of your dreams right now?"

"Well, that would definitely be the *Compact Oxford English Dictionary*, but, Dad—"

"Excuse me!" Dad called to Andrew over a rack of books. "One *Compact Oxford English Dictionary*, please!"

"Oh-kay," Andrew replied as he headed off to get the book.

"Dad, no. It costs a fortune!"

"You need something to remember this visit by," Dad insisted.

Dad's eyes widened when he saw the huge black box Andrew brought him.

"Here you go," Andrew said, panting a little beneath the weight.

"Holy mother of . . ." Dad took the book and held it up in front of him. "This is the monolith from *2001*!"

"It's got every word ever recorded in the English language, plus origins and earliest usage," I explained as we walked toward the register.

"You sure you wouldn't rather have a car?" he asked as he laid it on the counter. "They weigh about the same." He pulled out a gold card and handed it to Andrew. "Here you go."

I couldn't believe it. "This is so nice of you."

"Yeah, well, I've got a lot of things to make up for," he said softly.

"No, you don't."

"Yes, I do," he insisted.

Then Andrew came over. "Uh, I'm really sorry, Christopher," he whispered sheepishly, holding out Dad's credit card, "but your card's been—" He mouthed the final word—"*rejected*."

"Rejected?" Dad looked stunned. "What are you talking about?"

Andrew shrugged apologetically. "I could run it through again if you want."

"Yes," I said emphatically.

Dad reached for his card. "Uh . . . no." He looked at me, embarrassed. "He doesn't need to run it through again."

"Oh." I looked down at my hands. "Okay."

"Uh, could you maybe hold that for us?" Dad asked Andrew. "I'll come back tomorrow with another card?"

"Sure, Chris. No problem."

"Thanks. Come on," he said to me.

Outside we walked along in silence for a moment. Then Dad said, "Now you'll *really* remember me."

"I didn't want it that much anyway."

He slipped his arm around me and kissed me on top of the head.

Rory, during an evening inspired by Donna Reed

Lorelai in a snowy
Stars Hollow

Lorelai and Rory at a Friday night dinner

Rory at the Inn, sampling some of Sookie's freshly made desserts

Lorelai and Luke in Luke's Diner

Lorelai and Luke
taking a break from
painting the diner

Lorelai in her dad's study

The Family

Rory and Dean on their anniversary date

The Chilton
triumvirate—Paris,
Madeline, and Louise

Rory speaks out at a town meeting

❧

Grant, Official Stars Hollow troubadour

❧

Luke outside
his diner

❧

Tristin trying to lure Rory with PJ Harvey tickets

❧

Rory and Dean at the
"Black and White and Read" bookstore/theatre

"Hey, listen, don't tell your mom about this, okay?"

"Okay."

"Thanks."

We continued walking but stopped short when we heard a loud voice say, "Yes, it is her real dad."

We glanced up curiously at a crowd gathered on the corner, Jackson holding everyone's attention.

"He seems very nice, kind of a folky, poppy, urban scruffy look to him, obviously there's some money mixed in there because he's got that money nose and—"

Somebody cleared his throat, and Jackson broke off. He slowly turned around and smiled stiffly at us. Then he tipped his rolled stocking cap, not an easy feat, and took off down the street.

As Dad and I passed Luke's Diner, we spotted Mom sitting at a table in the window, reading and doing what she always does when she's in Luke's establishment: consuming a large cup of coffee.

We went in and joined her.

"Hey, where have you been?" Mom asked.

"Well, we saw Al's Paraguanian Pancake House, we were stalked by several townspeople, and I apparently look like Billy Crudup," Dad replied.

"You do not."

"Take it up with Jackson."

Just as we sat down, Dad's cell phone rang.

"Uhn, uh, uh, hey, hey, hey, hey!" Mom said as he reached for it. She pointed at a sign behind the counter that read: "No cell phones," accompanied by a large drawing of a cell phone inside a fat red circle with a slash through it. Luke doesn't appreciate the high technology.

Dad ignored the sign and answered anyway. Lucky for him Luke was in the back room.

"Hello? . . . Emily!"

"Emily?" Mom said.

"It's your mother," Dad whispered.

"Hi, Grandma!" I called out.

"Uh huh. Well, actually, I'm sitting here with your girls . . . sure." He held the phone out to Mom and grinned. "She wants to speak to you."

Dad and I looked at the menu while Mom talked to Grandma. We weren't paying attention to what she was saying but we knew it wasn't good when she hung up. Grandma wants to host a family reunion of sorts at our next Friday dinner, inviting Dad and his parents. This would be the first time we would be together as far back as I could remember, which was sort of exciting for me, but judging by their reactions, Mom and Dad didn't share that sentiment.

❦7

On Friday night the three of us stood outside the door to my grandparents' house. Mom and Dad looked great—Dad in his suit and tie and Mom with her snug black sweater over a Chinese-inspired red silk skirt.

Mom took a deep breath. "I've got to see my parents."

Dad sighed. "I've got to see my parents."

"Ladies and gentlemen," I announced, "the drama king and queen of Connecticut."

Mom took another deep breath and moved forward. She didn't ring or knock, like we normally did, but used her key to unlock the door.

"Hello? Anyone home?" she called out as we walked into the house.

Grandma rushed into the foyer, confused by our entrance. "Oh my God. You're here! Christopher, look at you!"

She hugged my dad with great affection.

"Emily, as always, perfect," he said gallantly.

"I am so glad to see you," Grandma went on. "I didn't hear the doorbell."

"We didn't ring the doorbell," Mom said.

"You let yourselves in?" Grandma looked surprised.

"It's okay, Mom. Look. Not a rapist among us."

"Hi, Grandma."

We handed our coats to the maid.

"You usually knock."

"Not since you gave us a key."

"That's for emergencies."

"Well, Mom, I'm starving to death. Is that enough of an emergency for you?"

Grandma gave Mom a pointed look, but was too much of a hostess to have a scene in front of a guest, so she put on a happy smile. "Richard's in the living room. Come on in. He's dying to see you."

Grandma led the way, and I followed. Behind me I could hear Mom muttering. "She set me up by giving me that key. The key is meant to be used. It's my parents' house."

My dad was clearly amused. "Shut up!" she said before Dad could say a word.

"Well, here they are," Grandpa said.

"Hi, Grandpa."

"Hello, Rory. Lorelai. Christopher, old boy, how are you?" He came over and shook Dad's hand. "My God, it's good to see you!"

"How are you, Richard?"

"Oh, better than most, not as good as some."

"And annoyed with all," Dad added.

"Ha-hah! You speak the truth, young man." He headed toward the bar. "I have made martinis."

"So, Christopher, tell me about your business," Grandpa said as he handed him two glasses.

"Oh, Richard. Let the poor boy relax," Grandma admonished him as Dad handed her a drink.

"Well, I simply want to know how it's going."

Grandpa handed Dad another glass, which he passed on to Mom before sitting down.

"It is going great, Richard," Dad said cheerfully. "I'm almost afraid to jinx it by telling you how good it's going."

"Oh, that is wonderful. I always knew you had it in you. You have a splash of greatness, as my mother would say. You always had that splash of greatness." He took a seat in his favorite chair by the fire and took a sip of his martini.

Mom had already drained hers and got up to refill her glass. "Yeah, I'd like another splash of greatness right here if you don't mind."

For a moment my grandparents just sat there, beaming at me and my dad.

"Oh, Richard," Grandma said proudly. "Isn't Rory the spitting image of Christopher?"

"I just hope you've inherited your father's business sense also, my dear," Grandpa said.

"I know one thing for sure," Grandma said. "You certainly have your father's musical talent."

"Oh, now wait just a minute," Mom said as she sat back down beside me.

"What?" Grandma asked.

"Neither of these two has *any* musical talent."

"Hey," Dad protested, "I play guitar."

Mom looked skeptical. "You know the opening lick to 'Smoke on the Water.'"

"And I've since mastered the opening lick to 'Jumpin' Jack Flash,'" Dad replied.

"I'm a Chuck Berry man myself," Grandpa offered.

Mom nearly choked on her drink.

"Something wrong?" Grandpa asked.

"I would never have guessed that that last sentence would ever come out of your mouth," Mom said.

"And why not?"

"Chuck Berry."

"Yes, Chuck Berry. He was all the rage when I was in school," Grandpa said defensively.

"So we're talking pre–'My Ding-a-Ling'?"

"I believe I am."

Grandma leaned forward, smiling. "Do you remember when the two of you were, what, ten, and you put on that adorable show for us?"

"What show, Mom?" my mom asked.

Dad chuckled. "Lucy, Schroeder, you lying on the coffee table—"

"You pretending it was a piano . . . right." Mom continued, "Oh God. Why is that remembered?"

"Because it was such a wonderful production!" Grandma exclaimed.

"Well, I don't know if it was a production, Mom. It was just one song."

She and Dad started laughing as they recalled the experience.

"'Suppertime,'" Dad said.

"Did you write that?" Grandpa exclaimed. "That was really very good."

"Dad! That's from *You're a Good Man, Charlie Brown*. It's a famous musical."

"Well, I thought Christopher might have written it. He's a very talented man."

The doorbell rang.

Grandma's face broke into a huge smile and she rose gracefully to her feet. "*That* would be Strobe and Francine."

As she went to answer the door, Mom leaned back and taunted Dad quietly. "Ha ha. Your turn."

"Haven't seen your parents in quite a number of years," Grandpa said cheerfully. "We were practically inseparable for a while." He set down his drink and also went to the door.

"This is weird," I said to my parents. "These are my other grandparents. I don't even know them. What do I call them?"

"Call 'em what I call 'em," Dad said, loosening his tie. "Ass—"

Mom cut him off. "*Chris!*"

"Sorry. My tie's too tight."

"Just call them . . . Strobe and Francine," Mom suggested. "Call them Mr. and Mrs. Haden. Sir and ma'am? Why don't you just avoid calling them anything?"

And then suddenly Grandpa was leading them into the room. "Look who's here!" he announced.

We all jumped to our feet.

My Dad's dad was short, with white hair and beard, slightly balding on the top. His mom was very chic in an ice-blue silk cocktail suit, her dark hair twisted into a French twist.

"Hello, Mother. Pop."

"Christopher." Mr. Haden shook Dad's hand.

"Christopher. Hello." Mrs. Haden straightened Dad's tie.

"Mr. and Mrs. Haden. Long time no see," Mom said brightly.

"Lorelai." She turned and looked Mom up and down. "You look well." But her smile was stiff.

"I am. Thanks. You remember Rory? You haven't seen her in quite a long time."

"No, we haven't," Mr. Haden said.

"I think she was just starting to speak in complete sentences," Mrs. Haden said.

"So not for two years, then?"

Mr. Haden cleared his throat, and he and his wife exchanged an uneasy look.

So did Grandma and Grandpa.

Mom kept going. "See, she's obviously been talking a long time, so I was actually making a humorous type of comment sometimes referred to as a joke."

"I see you haven't changed, Lorelai," Mr. Haden said.

"No. Not at all."

"Rory, hello," Mrs. Haden said with a lovely smile. And then everyone was staring at me and I got really uncomfortable. I didn't know what to do so I did a little curtsy as I said hello. Mom stifled a laugh.

"Did you . . . did you just curtsy?" Mom whispered.

"Shut up!" I whispered back.

"Sorry, milady."

"Strobe, Francine, how about a martini?" Grandpa asked his guests.

"Please," Mr. Haden replied.

He and Grandpa prepared the drinks as we sat down. "Well, Strobe, how is retirement treating you?" Grandpa asked.

"Yes, do tell us about the Bahamas," Grandma said.

"You can own an entire island there for the cost of a decent house here," Mr. Haden said.

"Really?"

"How about you, Richard. Any thoughts of retirement crossing your mind?"

Grandpa just laughed and waved him off.

"Oh, Strobe, if only you could talk him into it," Grandma said. "I've given up."

"We're very pleased to hear about Christopher's business success out in California," Grandpa said as he sat down in his usual chair, with Mr. Haden beside him on the couch.

Dad's dad nodded. "Yes. It's taken a long time, but it seems to be finally coming together. Seems to be."

Beside me, Dad started tugging at his collar.

"Christopher, your tie," his mom said. "Please."

I decided it was time to say something. I cleared my throat. "Strobe and Fran . . . Mr. and Mrs. Hay . . . Sir . . . Are you enjoying your time here? You . . . two?"

"That she got from you," Dad whispered to Mom behind me.

"How old are you now, young lady?" Mr. Haden asked.

"Sixteen."

"Dangerous age for girls," Mr. Haden muttered to his wife.

"Strobe," Mrs. Haden warned quietly.

"Rory is a very special child," Grandma jumped in. "Excellent student. Very bright."

"You should have a talk with her, Strobe." Grandpa chuckled. "She could give you a run for your money."

"Is that so?" Mr. Haden said.

"That's right," Grandma agreed proudly.

I smiled back. Their praise meant a lot to me.

Then everyone stared at me again. Waiting for me to say something clever. Waiting for me to make Mr.

Haden run for his money. My mind went totally blank.
I glanced helplessly at Mom and Dad.

"Well, I think my money's safe," Mr. Haden said ar-
rogantly.

I felt Mom stiffen beside me.

"I hate President Bush!" Mom blurted out.

"What?!" Mr. Haden exclaimed incredulously.

"Lorelai . . ." Grandma said sternly.

Dad dropped his head. "Oh boy."

"He's stupid and his face is too tiny for his head and
I just want to toss him out."

"That is the leader of our country, young lady!" Mr.
Haden said hotly.

Grandpa was leaning his head in his hand, with a "here
we go" look on his face. "Ignore her," he implored Strobe.

"His face is too tiny for his head?" Mrs. Haden said,
stunned. "What kind of thing is that to say?"

"I see your daughter's just as out of control as ever,
Richard," Mr. Haden said.

Grandpa sat up.

"Pop, please!" Dad said. "Let's keep it civil."

But Mr. Haden ignored him. "Tell me, Lorelai," he said
harshly. "What have you been doing with your life anyway, besides hating successful businessmen? I'm just
curious."

"Why don't we all go into the dining room?"
Grandma said brightly.

"Well, uh . . . Strobe," Mom replied, "I run an inn,
near Stars Hollow."

"Really."

"Yes, *really*."

"Dad, come on," my dad said.

"Nice to see you've found your calling," Mr. Haden
said disdainfully.

"Dinner's ready!" Grandma said desperately.

Dad started fiddling with his tie again.

"Christopher, your tie!" his mother repeated.

"Mom, please!"

"And is your life everything that you hoped it would be?" Mr. Haden continued.

"Yes, it is."

"Because it seems to me you might not want to take *quite* such a haughty tone when you announce to the world that you work in a hotel."

"Well, there's nothing wrong with where I work—"

"Strobe, please," Mrs. Haden said. "I'm getting a headache."

"Come on, Richard," Grandma insisted. "Lead us into the dining room. *Now*."

But Mr. Haden pressed on, his voice bitter and hard. "If you'd attended a university, as your parents had planned, and as we planned in vain for Christopher, you might have aspired to something more than a blue-collar position."

"Don't do this," Dad said.

Mom just sat there, arms crossed over her lap, controlling her anger.

"And I wouldn't give a damn about you derailing your own life if you hadn't swept my son along with you!" Mr. Haden continued.

Mom turned to me. "Honey, go in the next room," She said calmly. "Go, go."

I left the room, but I could still hear every word being said. Grandpa spoke up. "I'm going to have to echo Christopher's call for civility here. A mutual mistake was made many years ago by these two, but they've both come a long way since."

"A mutual mistake, Richard?" Mr. Haden retorted.

"This whole evening is ridiculous." "We're supposed to sit around here like one big happy family and pretend that the damage that was done is over? Gone? I don't care about how good a student you say that girl is!"

"Hey—!" Mom jumped in.

"Our son was bound for Princeton!" Mr. Haden continued. "Every Haden male has attended Princeton, including myself, but it all stopped with Christopher. It's a humiliation we've had to live with every day—all because you *seduced* him into ruining his life! She had that baby and she ended his future!"

"You recant that, Strobe," Grandpa said angrily. "You owe my daughter an apology!"

"An apology! That is rich."

I glanced back into the living room to see what was happening just as Grandpa jumped up, his voice surged in outrage. "How dare you! How dare you!" He grabbed Dad's dad by the lapels and started shaking him.

"Richard, what are you doing?" Grandma said, completely in shock.

"Let go of me!"

"How dare you come into my house and insult my daughter like that!"

"I said let go of me!"

"Whoa, whoa! What is happening here?" Dad jumped between the two men and tried to separate them.

"Shame on you, Strobe!" Grandpa said angrily. "Shame on you for opening all this up again."

"Get your purse, Francine!" Mr. Haden ordered his wife.

"My daughter is very successful at what she does!"

"We're leaving," Mr. Haden said.

"You're not leaving!" Grandpa shouted. "I'm kicking you out!"

Grandpa marched toward the foyer. Mr. Haden followed him. Ever poised, Mrs. Haden stood, handed Grandma her martini glass, clutched her purse to her side, and exited the room. Grandma went out after them.

Mom and Dad stood together in front of the fire, totally stunned. Mom was holding Dad's arm.

They just stared. "And you brought up Bush because . . . ?"

"It seemed like a good idea at the time? Wow."

"Yeah."

"I feel . . . sixteen."

I shrank back into the kitchen. I had seen way too much.

8

Grandpa retreated to his study and everyone else just seemed to disappear, dinner forgotten. I stayed in the kitchen and Grandma and Grandpa's maid put the food away.

A short while later, Grandma breezed into the kitchen. "Oh, there you are! I was wondering where you went."

"Sorry."

"No, it's nothing to be sorry about." She bustled about the room. "Can I get you something?"

"I'm fine." I held up the soda I had just opened.

"Oh, that's hardly dinner." She opened their huge refrigerator and began pulling out all the food their maid had just put away. "Well, there was quite a bit of excitement tonight," she said with a big smile.

"Oh yeah."

"Not the good kind."

"Nope."

She looked at me a long moment, and then her voice softened. "None of this means anything, Rory."

"Oh, I know."

"Strobe is actually a good man, very smart." She got a plate and began dishing out enough food to feed a couple of football players. "He was one of the top lawyers in his field, a very arcane aspect of international law, and he's always been so active in his community. His charity work has never diminished over the years."

I nodded politely. Suddenly the plate dropped on the counter.

"Oh, let's face it!" Grandma said, letting her guard down. "He's a big *ass*."

I looked up, surprised, then laughed.

Grandma sat down on the stool across from me.

"Rory, I know you heard a lot of talk about various disappointments this evening. And I know you've heard a lot of talk about it in the past. But I want to make this very clear." She looked me hard in the eye. "You, young lady, your person and your existence, have never ever been, not even for a second, included in that list." She paused to let it sink in. "Do you understand me?"

I smiled at her. "Yeah. I do."

"Good!" She smiled and held out my plate. "Now eat up."

∽

I spent the rest of the evening with Grandma. Mom and Dad finally emerged from wherever they'd disappeared to and we piled into Mom's Jeep to head home. Dad drove.

My parents were uncharacteristically quiet.

"So, where were you guys?" I asked.

"Nowhere," Mom answered a little too quickly.

"Where's nowhere?" I pressed.

"Where we were," Dad answered.

"Um hmm," Mom said, so softly I could barely hear her.

"Ahhh," I said. I was obviously not going to get anything out of them so I dropped the subject.

No one said another word the rest of the way home.

When we got into the house, Dad gave me a kiss and told me good night.

I watched Mom and Dad say good night to each other, but things seemed strained.

Dad smiled at me and headed into the living room.

I peered at Mom in the bright hall light. "You've got some dirt or schmutz or something here." I reached up and tried to wipe off her face. "Where did you—"

She didn't let me finish my sentence. "Look, it was a long night. A lot of schmoozing going on."

"Okay."

"Hey, come here. We haven't really had a chance to talk." She led me into the kitchen.

"About the schmoozing?"

"No. About all the warm and fuzzy family moments that went on tonight." She tossed her pocketbook on the counter and peered into my face. "Are you okay?"

"Yeah, I'm fine."

"You know, all those crazy people saying horrible things were directing them at me. Not you."

"They were directing them at you because you had me," I corrected.

"*No*. They were directing them at me because I screwed up their big Citizen Kane plans. That's all."

Suddenly, everything that happened that night hit me and I caught a glimpse of the life Mom left behind. "They don't even want to know me, do they?" I said, trying to swallow the hurt.

"That is not true!" Mom said. "They are just so full of anger and stupid pride that . . . it stands in the way of them realizing how much they want to know you."

"Yeah." I shrugged.

"Their loss," Mom said. "And it's a pretty big one."

I sighed. "I'm going to go to bed now."

I headed toward my room. I had a lot to think about.

"Hey," Mom called out.

I turned.

"No regrets," she said. "Not from me or from your dad."

"Yeah?" I said, feeling a little better.

"Well, I mean, no regrets about you. There is a misspelled tattoo incident that I'm sure he'd love to erase from his bio, but you, that's a no-brainer."

"Where does Dad have a misspelled tattoo?"

"Uh uh! Another story for another time. Possibly before your first trip to Mazatlán. Good night, babe."

"Good night, Mom."

∽

Early the next morning Dad was on his bike in front of our house. It was a gorgeous day, chilly, with a bright sun in a bright blue sky. But I hardly noticed.

Dad was leaving.

"So call us when you get home," Mom said as we stood side by side watching him.

"I will."

"And call more," I added.

He grinned. "I will."

"See you."

"Drive safe."

He hugged and kissed me goodbye. Then he whispered in my ear.

I smiled and walked over to Mom.

"Dad wants to know if you'll reconsider."

Mom's smile was bittersweet and she waved me over so she could give me her answer.

"She says, 'Nope, Offspring sucks and Metallica rules,'" I relayed to Dad.

"Fair enough," he replied.

Then he and Mom hugged. And I looked on sadly.

"Drive safe," she whispered.

Dad pulled on his helmet and drove away.

I watched until he disappeared, then turned to Mom.

"He wanted you to marry him, didn't he?" I said softly.

"Spy."

"You know, crazier things have happened," I pointed out.

"You mean crazier than having your mom and dad married?"

"Yes."

"I don't think they have."

"What? Why is that crazy?" I couldn't believe she was letting him go.

"Because it is," Mom said, struggling for words. "Because he's . . . he wants things that he's not ready for."

"How do you know?"

"I know. I know him so well." And now she was choking back tears. "You have no idea."

"Maybe he can change," I argued.

"Rory . . ."

"Maybe it's different," I insisted. "He did come here this time. He's never done that before . . ."

"Hey, stop."

"Why?"

Mom's face looked pained. "Because I don't want you getting yourself all worked up over this."

"He loves you," I said.

"He does love me."

"Do you love him?" I asked.

Mom looked away. "Honey, come on—"

"Answer me." I really wanted to know.

"Honestly?"

"Yes."

Mom sighed. "I will probably always love him."

"Okay, so . . . ?"

"But that doesn't change the fact that he has a long way to go before he's ready to take us on full time. I mean, you are a handful, missy, and while I am pure joy and sunshine every waking hour, I still have my own set of needs that must be met. It just wasn't right, babe. You have to trust me on that."

We turned around to walk back to the house. I didn't say anything.

Mom gave my arm a gentle shake. "Talk, please."

"I still think there was a little something different," I muttered.

"Maybe you're right."

"Really?"

"It would be nice."

"Yeah, it would."

"I'll tell you what," Mom said with a smile, "let's not put all the blankets away just yet."

"Really?" I said, hopeful.

She looked back over her shoulder at the road. "You never know."

∽9

Even though my dad had only been with us for a few days, I had grown used to having him around, and it felt a little odd without him. Fortunately I had the distraction of the Stars Hollow Founders Firelight Festival.

The streets were filled with people getting ready for our town's biggest celebration, an old-fashioned event that celebrates the lovers that founded our town.

As my bus from Chilton pulled into town passing Miss Patty's dance studio, I saw her leaning in the doorway smoking a cigarette, telling a group of kids the tale of our founders' forbidden love and the magic that brought them to our town. I could almost hear her tell the story as I had heard it over and over so many years before:

This, boys and girls, is a story of true love. A beautiful girl from one county, a handsome boy from another, they meet, and they fell in love. Separated by distance and by parents who did not approve of the union, the young couple dreamed of the day

*that they could be together. They wrote each other beautiful let-
ters, letters of longing and passion, letters full of promises and
plans for the future. Soon the separation proved too much for
either one of them to bear. So, one night, cold and black with no
light to guide them, they both snuck out of their homes and ran
away as fast as they could. It was so dark out that they were
both soon lost and it seemed as if they would never find each
other. Finally, the girl dropped to her knees, tears streaming
down her lovely face. "Oh, my love, where are you? How will I
find you?" Suddenly, a band of stars appeared in the sky. These
stars shone so brightly they lit up the entire countryside.*

*The girl jumped to her feet and followed the path of the stars
until finally she found herself standing right where the town
gazebo is today. There waiting for her was her one true love, who
had also been led here by the blanket of friendly stars.*

The bus pulled up to the stop and I saw Dean in his
black leather coat sitting on the back of the bench, feet
planted squarely on the green wooden seat, reading the
paperback copy of *Anna Karenina* I had loaned him. He
frowned slightly, studying the page, totally engrossed in
Tolstoy's tragic romantic epic.

I got off the bus and approached Dean, eager to hear
what he thought of one of my all-time favorite books.

"So?" I greeted him.

Dean took a deep breath and searched for words to
express what he was feeling. "It's . . ." He grimaced.
". . . depressing," he said at last.

"It's *beautiful*!" I responded.

"She throws herself under a *train*."

"But I bet she looked great doing it." I slid my yellow
backpack off my shoulders and climbed up on the back
of the bench beside him.

Dean shrugged apologetically. "I don't know. I think
maybe Tolstoy's just a little over my head."

"No, that's not true! Tolstoy wrote for the masses," I insisted. "The common man. It's completely untrue that you have to be some kind of genius to read his stuff."

Dean shifted uncomfortably. "Yeah, but—"

"Now, I know it's big . . ."

"Very big."

"And long . . ."

"Very, *very* long."

". . . and many of the Russian names tend to be spelled very similar and therefore can lead to confusion," I admitted.

"Every single person's name ends with 'sky'!" he exclaimed. "How is that possible?"

"But it's one of my favorite books," I said, trying to persuade him, "and I know that if you just gave it a chance you'd—"

"All right. I'll try again," he said, making a valiant effort not to look miserable at the prospect.

"Really?" He was going to read a huge book that he hated—just for me. Now, that was romantic. I smiled and gazed into his beautiful dark eyes.

He sent the gaze right back. "Yes."

"You won't be sorry."

"Coffee?" he suggested.

"Please."

We climbed off the bench and slung our backpacks over our shoulders.

"Man," Dean said as he looked around the square at the major preparations going on for the festival. "And I thought *Christmas* was a big deal around here."

He was right. People stood on ladders hanging up papier-mâché stars the size of piñatas. Hundreds of small silver stars fluttered in the trees. Star-spangled garlands and tinsel draped every porch railing and storefront in sight. Booths were being set up to sell star-shaped food and star-shaped souvenirs. Tiny white lights strung everywhere would sparkle like a million tiny stars after dark. Hanging from every lamppost was the official Founders Firelight Festival poster of two silhouetted lovers meeting in front of a beautiful fire under a sky full of stars.

"Well, this is a town that really enjoys the celebrating," I said. "Last year we had a month-long carnival when we finally got off the septic tank system."

Dean's jaw dropped. "Month long? You're kidding."

"No," I replied. "There were rides, and a petting zoo, and balloon animals, and a freak show . . ."

Dean laughed, realizing I was teasing him.

"Uh oh. Okay, you almost had me going there for a minute."

I grinned. "Well, we did have a ribbon-cutting ceremony."

We continued walking, weaving our way through the boxes and people cluttering the sidewalks. Dean took a deep breath.

"So, uh, what are you doing Friday night?" he asked.

"Well, I've got the usual Friday night grandparents' dinner." He grimaced, so I quickly added, "But I thought maybe if we get back here early enough you and I could watch some of the bonfire together. I mean, it's a little corny, but it's really pretty." I nudged him for the final sale. "And they sell star-shaped hot dogs."

Dean grinned. "How about if you *get out* of dinner at your grandparents' this week?"

"I don't think so," I said reluctantly.

"But what if it's for a *really* special occasion?" I couldn't imagine what he had in mind. There was nothing going on in Stars Hollow on Friday night that wasn't related to the Founders Firelight Festival.

"Well, that special occasion had better include me being permanently relocated to a plastic bubble for my grandmother to let me out of dinner," I said.

"There *must* be some other excuse you could use," Dean persisted.

"Like what?"

"Like ... it's your three-month anniversary with your boyfriend?" he stated, avoiding my eyes.

It was the last thing in the world I'd expected. I stopped walking. "It is?"

Dean turned around, hands in his pockets, and looked at me.

"Yeah," he said. "Three months from your birthday. That's when I gave you the bracelet and that's when I figure this whole thing kind of started."

I was stunned. I hadn't even remembered. "Wow. Three months," was all I could say.

"Actually, *technically* your birthday was on a Saturday, so it really should be Saturday"—he was talking nonstop now—"but I work Saturday and I planned out this whole big thing. . . . So I thought maybe we could do it on Friday." He stopped and smiled hopefully.

I stared at him. "*What* whole big thing?"

He ignored my question and stepped closer. "Just this once," he said softly. "Miss dinner. Please? Don't make me throw myself under a train."

How could I say no? "I'll see what I can do."

Dean smiled. "Thank you."

"You're welcome."

"It's our three-month anniversary," I repeated.

"Yes, it is."

"I feel kind of stupid that I didn't even know about this."

"That's quite all right," Dean replied.

"And I feel *really* bad that I missed our *two*-month anniversary," I said.

"That's quite all right too."

"How was it?"

He grinned. "Pretty good."

I grinned back. "I'm glad."

We continued down the sidewalk, both grinning ear to ear. We passed the town troubadour, Grant, as he leaned against a decorated lamppost. He was strumming his acoustic guitar and singing a song I think is called "Heavenly." The lyrics went something like, "Heavenly, heavenly, no other love was meant to be mine." It's eerie how his songs always seem to fit my life perfectly whenever I pass him.

∽

When I got home later that afternoon, I found Mom sitting in the kitchen staring at a box of Hamburger Helper.

I slapped my hands down on the kitchen table and looked her straight in the eye. "No," I said firmly. "Put that away."

"But I want to cook!" she whined.

Okay, so I know there are people all over this great nation for whom this is not a big issue. People who love spending four hours making meat sauce for their pasta, who take the time to wash, chop and fry, who make cinnamon ice cream from scratch. People who thrill at the challenge of doing it all. Who find it far more satisfying than devouring Chinese out of cardboard boxes. People like Sookie, who dream of sauces and sautéing even as they sleep.

But my mom does not cook. And since *she* doesn't cook, she never taught *me* how to cook, and since they don't have Home Ec at Chilton, this genetic mutation could go on for generations in the Gilmore women.

Come to think of it, Grandma doesn't cook either. She simply hires people to cook for her. This thing may go back even further than I realized.

Now Mom was intrigued by her box of Hamburger Helper. I had to stop her before it was too late. "You can make soup," I sternly informed her. Cans we know how to open.

"No!" She grabbed the box. "I want to *really* cook, like on the Food Channel. I want to sauté things and chop things and do the *bam!* and arrange things on a plate so they look like a pretty little hat." Her eyes flashed. "I want to be the Iron Chef!"

I sighed. You can't stop Lorelai Gilmore when she has her heart set on something. "Fine," I said.

Her eyes lit up. "Really?"

"Yes. I'll help."

"Okay, good." She stared at the back of the package, frowning as she read the directions. "I need . . . a *pan*," she said.

"And a fire extinguisher."

"Funny, funny girl."

I opened the oven, which we use for storage since we don't use it for cooking, and looked for an appropriate-sized skillet.

"Okay." Mom read more of the recipe, then bit her lip. "Now . . . if I'd only bought some hamburger . . ."

I stared at her in amazement. "You didn't buy *hamburger*?"

"Yes, I bought hamburger! I just like saying stuff that makes you look at me like I'm crazy." She got up and began to dig through the fridge.

I just shook my head and kept looking. No luck in the stove, so I started digging through the cupboards. "So, tell me, why the sudden need to be domestic?"

"I don't know," Mom said. "I'm just sort of in a funky mood."

"Why?"

"Too many stars. Too much love! It makes me cranky."

Now, generally, Mom loves the idea of love. And Stars Hollow was in the throes of its annual glut of romance and love with this festival. Even old married couples who fought fifty-one weeks out of the year fell into a lovey-dovey swoon during this particular week.

Mom was feeling left out.

"I take it you haven't heard from Mr. Medina," I ventured.

"No, I haven't." Mom sat down at the table and plopped the package of ground beef next to the Hamburger Helper box.

"Maybe that's why you're cranky," I suggested.

"Okay," she said brightly. "New subject, please."

"You know," I continued, in spite of the evil eye, "you have a phone also."

"Hey, how's it coming with that pan?" she said, smacking her hands together.

I shook my head. "Cleopatra, Queen of Denial . . ."

Mom shot me a look. "The pan, Shecky, please."

"Okay, fine. New topic."

"Thank you."

I slid into the chair across from her. "I have this huge favor to ask you."

Mom's eyes lit up and she rubbed her hands together in delight. "Oooh, something I can hold over your head. Let's hear it."

"Friday night is Dean's and my three-month anniversary."

Mom blinked. Not what she was expecting. "Three months? Wow." She took a sip of coffee.

"And Dean apparently has some big fancy evening planned for us," I went on.

"Very classy of him," Mom said.

"Yes, it is. But for me to actually partake of the foresaid fancy evening . . ." I took a deep breath and rushed out, "I need to get out of Friday night dinner."

The playfulness of our exchange died an instant death.

"Ah," Mom said.

"Yes," I said.

"Well, good luck with *that*."

"*Mom!*"

She looked at me in exasperation. "Do you *know* how much Emily Gilmore will *not* care about your three-month anniversary?"

"I was thinking you could talk to her."

"If there was a runoff between what Emily Gilmore would care about less, a two-for-one toilet paper sale at Costco or your three-month anniversary, your anniversary would win hands down."

"So, you're not even going to try to help me?"

"Oh no, I am going to try to help you, because I care. Emily Gilmore, however—"

"Phone, please." Mom could go on for hours on the subject of her mother. But I didn't have that much time. I wanted action, now.

Mom threw up her hands in surrender. "Okay."

Mom braced herself, took a deep breath, then stood up, and laughed as she picked up the phone.

"What?"

"Nothing, just . . ." She began a mock conversation with Grandma as she punched out the phone number. "Oh, hey, Mom, Rory and Dean are having their three-month anniversary on Friday.

"Really, Lorelai?" she answered herself, doing an absolutely miserable imitation of Grandma's response. "Well that is *wonderful!* I'm *thrilled!*"

"Stop," I told her.

"Three months?" Mom as Grandma gushed. "Well, whoo-hoo! Hold on, I'm going to cartwheel!"

"Forget it."

"Oh! No, wait! She's telling my dad now," she continued to pretend.

"That's it. Find your own pan."

"*Hello?*" I barely heard Grandma's electrified voice coming over the phone line.

Mom instantly straightened like a chastised schoolgirl. "Mom?" she said into the phone. "Hi! How ya doin'?" Mom turned and started walking. She almost never sits still when she's talking to Grandma—it makes her too nervous. I followed her as she paced into the living room, trying to guess what Grandma was saying.

"Well, that's good," Mom was saying. "How's Dad? . . . Um, I just wanted to call to . . . to say hello."

"As a matter of fact, there is," she said into the

phone. "Well, see, you know Rory? She wanted to say hello too."

I groaned. Mom is usually pretty tough. She's made her own way in the world since I was born and has worked her way up from a job as a maid to a job managing a whole staff of not-easily-managed people at the Independence Inn. She can really kick butt—I've seen her do it millions of times. But Grandma can turn her into a blob of Jell-O with a single word.

"Okay, Mom," she said, "just hear me out, okay? Don't say anything. See, Friday night is Rory and Dean's three-month anniversary, and while that may not seem like a very big deal to you, it is to them. And I know that I'm going to ask you to do something that you are so not going to want to do, but I am begging you to look at it from her point of view, and maybe, just maybe let her, just this once, not come to dinner on Friday."

I held my breath.

Mom looked perplexed. Then she sat down on the couch. "What?" she said into the phone.

I crouched on my knees on the couch beside her. "Mom?" I whispered.

She ignored me. "Are you sure?"

I hated hearing only one side of this conversation.

"No arguments?" Mom asked, then frowned. "She won't be there . . . at all . . . the whole night long . . ." she clarified.

I held my breath. Dare I hope . . . ?

"All right," Mom said. She suddenly saw an opportunity and had to go with it. "You know, Mom, she's going to need a lot of help getting ready for the big night, so I should probably stay home and—"

Grandma cut her off.

"Right." Mom's shoulders sagged. "Okay. Bye."

Mom hung up and stared across the living room.

"So?" I asked eagerly.

She looked at me. "The world is officially coming to an end."

I looked at my mom, amazed. I was going out with Dean this Friday.

↜10

"Oh, we got new coffee makers. Ugh! What was I thinking?" Mom was frustrated. She'd been over at Luke's Diner earlier commiserating with Luke about how much they both hated Stars Hollow's Founders Firelight Festival and about how sickening the town's overblown love binge was.

And then Rachel walked in. A major blast from his past. His former significant other. I guess it kind of blew Mom's crab fest with him.

It was Friday night and Mom was helping me get ready for the big date. I was sitting in front of the dressing table mirror while she brushed my hair. Or yanked my hair.

"Ow! I'm still attached to the head, Mom."

"Sorry," Mom apologized, laying down the brush. "I'm just a little worked up."

"Mom, it's just Luke's ex-girlfriend," I reminded her.

She stopped brushing and started pinning my hair back. "I know that. I just hate that I made myself look so stupid in front of—"

"Luke?" I asked.

"No. Rachel," she corrected. "She was standing there, fresh off a plane, and she had no plane hair at all, might I add."

"What exactly is plane hair?" I asked.

"You know, it's all big, and all . . . blah. And he's looking at her like she's Miss September and she's looking at him like he's Johnny Depp; and I was just babbling like a complete moron. God, what is wrong with me." She began her frantic brushing again.

"Ow, ow." I held up my hands in self-defense. "Okay, you are now officially off hair duty."

"Oh, I'm sorry, honey, I just—"

"No, it's okay. I just think it's still a little early for Dean to see me completely bald."

"Right, that's more a six-month thing."

"So, what is going on with you?" I said seriously.

"I don't know. It's just all this love in the air, you know . . . I miss Max." She plopped down on my bed. "There's been so much going on with . . . your dad coming home, family stuff, and your constant existence . . ."

"Thanks for the love."

"Anytime. So . . . I haven't had a lot of time to focus on it and . . . I miss Max. I had a dream about him the other night."

"Really? Dirty?"

"No. Absolutely not. And when you turn twenty-one I'll tell you the real answer. But, I don't know, I've been in kind of a funk since then."

"I'm sorry."

"Me, too. We could talk about me for years, and believe me, we will, but let's focus on you, the lady of the evening, no hooker reference intended."

"Glad to hear it."

"Now, what are you gonna wear with that?" Mom asked.

I had on a cherry-red dress, knee-length, with bare shoulders. I held up a couple of sweaters. "You tell me."

Mom studied them. "Well, where is he taking you?"

"Why?"

"Because you don't want to clash with the décor. A lady plans ahead."

"Well," I said, "if you must know, he's taking me to Andoloro's."

"Oh, isn't *that* romantic!" Mom said.

"I know!"

"Wow. It's going to be just like *Lady and the Tramp*! You'll share a plate of spaghetti, but it'll just be one long strand but you won't realize it until you accidentally meet in the middle. And then he'll push a meatball toward you with his nose. And you'll push it back with your nose. And then you'll bring the meatball home and save it in the refrigerator for years, and—"

"Mom?" I interrupted, holding up the two sweaters, reminding her I needed to get dressed.

"Neither," Mom decided. "Just wear your coat."

"Okay."

"But your flower's just a little smushed." She came over and adjusted the fabric flower on the neck of my dress. I heard Lane call out as she came through the front door.

"There, all set," Mom said. She seemed a little sad.

"Are you all right?" I asked softly.

"Oh yeah!" She waved me off. "You look beautiful. Go."

I hurried out to meet Lane in the entryway.

"I just can't believe it!" she squealed when she saw me.

"I know!"

"I mean, three months!" she exclaimed. "That's like one sixty-fourth of your life!"

"I know!"

"I have to stop hanging out with you," she stated as we headed to the living room. "You're just making my life seem too pathetic."

"Join the club," Mom joked as we passed.

"Are you going to go to the festival?" I asked her. "'Cause maybe we could meet you there later."

"Oh yeah, that would be romantic."

"Lane."

We sat down in the living room for a moment. "Yes, I am going to the festival and would you like to know why? My mother has once again set me up."

"Another future doctor?"

"A future chiropractor. I think she's losing confidence in my prospects."

"Maybe he'll be nice."

"Oh, it's not just him. We're going with his parents, his grandparents, two sisters, three brothers, and at least one maiden aunt."

A horn honked in the street. "That's Dean!"

Lane grinned and walked me to the front door. "Remember, you have to tell me everything."

"Okay. You too," I told her.

"Oh yeah. After the walking, the silence, the sitting, and the buh-bye, that's when the fun will begin."

"I want to know anyhow." I turned and gave my mother a hug. "Bye, Mom."

"Bye, honey, have fun."

I threw on my coat and grabbed my purse.

"Don't forget the meatball!" She winked.

Lane frowned. "The meatball?"

"It's a mother-daughter thing," Mom replied.

I smiled at her, waved, and ran out the door.

The restaurant was small, intimate, very classy. Perfect.

Dean looked wonderful in a dark brown turtleneck and candlelight. He spent the entire evening trying to make everything perfect for me.

"That was really good," I said when the waiter cleared away our meal.

Dean looked anxious. "It was?"

"Yes, it was."

"How was the salad?"

"Great."

"What about that cheesebread thing? Too heavy?"

"Just heavy enough."

"Really?"

"Everything was perfect," I assured him. "Even the soda was good. I don't know how they do it, but the Coke here is definitely superior to the Coke anywhere else."

"Okay . . ." Dean leaned forward on the table. "At what point during that did you start making fun of me?"

"I would never make fun of you," I insisted. "Especially not after you ordered three different kinds of pasta for me just because I couldn't decide."

"Well, you shouldn't have to decide," Dean said. "I mean, tonight you should have everything you want."

I looked into his eyes. "I just have to say, I am now a very big fan of the three-month anniversary."

"Oh yeah?"

"Definitely. I think they should have T-shirts and newsletters."

"I'm glad."

"You did all this for me."

He smiled. "It's not over yet."

"Wow," I said, shaking my head. "This is just like that Christmas that I got a full set of illustrated encyclopedias."

Dean stared at me, a little lost.

"No! I *wanted* them!" I clarified.

"Oh, good."

Just then the waiter came over with our dessert. "One tiramisu, two forks, and . . ." He chuckled and held up a paper bag. "One meatball to go."

"Thank you." I smiled and placed the bag beside my purse.

"You want to explain the meatball?" Dean asked.

I shrugged. "It's a mother-daughter thing."

"Okay." He waved at the dessert. "Well, ladies first."

"Thank you."

I picked up my fork and took a bite. It was delicious. "Okay, have I mentioned how much I'm loving this three-month anniversary thing?"

"Yeah, you did."

"Because this tiramisu is so good that if the anniversary were completely sucking right now, this would save it."

He grinned and leaned back in his chair and just looked at me.

"What?" I said.

"Nothing."

"Stop it."

"No, you look cute."

"I'm eating."

"Well, you eat cute."

"I do not eat cute. No one eats cute. Bambi maybe, but he's a cartoon."

"So, after we finish here," he said, leaning forward, "we move on to phase two of the anniversary evening."

"Phase two. Sounds very official. Are there space suits involved."

"With matching helmets."

"Impressive."

I wondered what else he had planned, but Dean just took a bite of dessert and wouldn't say any more.

After dinner we strolled toward Dean's truck holding hands. People were pouring into the streets to celebrate, mostly happy couples, arm in arm.

"So, what book did you bring?" Dean asked as we crossed the street.

"What?"

"Come on. You always bring a book with you, and I'm just wondering what was the three-month-anniversary book?"

"Actually I brought *The New Yorker*."

"A magazine. Really."

"It's the fiction issue," I defended.

As we passed the gazebo in the center of town, Stars Hollow's mayor, Harrison Porter, flanked by Taylor Doose and Miss Patty, stepped up to the podium. "People of Stars Hollow and our many friends!" he announced. "It is my great pleasure to preside over our annual Founders' Firelight Festival for the thirty-second time."

The large crowd of people who had gathered, bundled up in hats and coats and snuggled together in the cold, applauded.

"Many a true love has had its start right on the spot where I now stand," the mayor went on. "And I don't mind telling you that it was during this very festival, right by the gazebo, that I met my only true love, Miss Dora Braithwaite!"

There was a sprinkling of applause.

"We've been married forty-three years," the mayor said proudly, "and it all started right here."

Taylor covered the mike. "Ask her to wave."

Mayor Porter shifted uncomfortably. "I *can't*."

"Why not?"

"She went to bingo in Bridgeport," the mayor whispered, then turned back to the crowd.

"And now, my friends," the mayor went on, "if you will join me in lighting the fire!"

I took Dean's hand and said, "Okay, take me to the surprise now."

Dean looked confused. "But Mayor Porter just said—"

"Trust me, it's going to be a while before it's lit. We'll be back in plenty of time."

Up on the stand, Mayor Porter, Taylor Doose, and Miss Patty were searching through their pockets.

"Every damn year!" the mayor said.

Dean and I hurried past the gazebo.

"It was Lenny's responsibility," Taylor stated.

"Oh, for Pete's sake!" the mayor muttered. He looked at the crowd. "Does anybody have any matches?"

∽

"We're here," Dean announced as we stopped in front of a chain-link fence.

"We're where?"

"Come on," Dean said, excited.

I glanced through the fence and saw rusted old cars. A lonesome-sounding dog barked mournfully in the distance. "Dean, what *is* this?"

"Okay," he said, "did you ever see *Christine*?" referring to the movie about a car with demonic powers. "Yes . . ." I replied.

"Well, it's nothing like that," Dean said. "Come *on*."

He opened the chained gate wide enough for us to slip through. I looked around at the piles of junk and dilapidated cars. "You brought me to Beirut?"

"It's a salvage yard," he said, leading me deeper into the ruins.

"Ah. And it looks so much like Beirut."

We passed the skeletons of dozens of old cars and finally stopped in front of a pile of metal decorated with shiny, rusting hubcaps and a lone string of lights.

"Okay," Dean said. "Here we are." He looked at me expectantly.

"Wow," I said, a little confused.

"It's a car," he explained.

I looked at the pile of metal. It was basically a frame with seats and a steering wheel. "It is?"

"Well," he said, "it will be."

"When it grows up?" I asked.

Dean laughed nervously. "When I . . . fix it."

"What?" I looked into his eyes. He was dead serious.

"Um, it's yours," he said.

"What do you mean, it's mine?"

"I mean, I've been building it, piece by piece, for . . . you."

"No —"

"Yeah! I—I started with the frame. The seats and the windshield just went in yesterday . . ."

"You're building me a car?"

"It's going to take a while, but when I'm done, it'll be great."

"You're building me a car." I stared at him in disbelief. "You're building *me* a car?"

"That's right."

"You're building me a car?"

"I'm building you a car."

"This is crazy!" I exclaimed, grinning. "Why would you do this?"

"I don't know. You didn't have one."

"You're completely insane!"

"What? I don't want you wasting time on the bus anymore. I mean, that is very valuable time that we could be arguing about your ongoing obsession with very confusing Russian authors."

"I can't believe this."

"Um . . . do you like it?"

"Do I like it? Are you kidding?" I threw my arms around him and gave him the biggest kiss of his life.

"I'll take that as a yes," Dean said when we finally parted.

I grinned. "Take it, mister."

"Come on, get in." He reached around and opened the door for me; it screeched as it came off its hinge and crashed to the ground.

"Uh, I'll fix that," Dean said hurriedly.

"Don't! I like it like that."

The seat was covered with an old plaid blanket Dean had laid out earlier, and I slid behind the wheel and admired the interior of my new—car.

Dean ran around to the other side, but the door

wouldn't open, so he hopped over it and slid into the seat beside me.

"This is amazing."

"I'm glad you like it."

"I had no idea three months was the car anniversary."

"Four months, you get a plane."

"Boy, relationships have sure changed since I was a kid."

Dean smiled and put his arm around me, and I curled up on his shoulder. Stars were twinkling in the sky above us. It was perfect.

"I'm having one of those moments," I whispered. "Right now."

"What moments?"

"One of those moments when everything is so perfect, and so wonderful, that you almost feel sad because nothing could ever be this good again."

"So," Dean said, "basically I'm depressing you."

"Yep."

"You're very weird."

"And you're wonderful."

We kissed softly and pulled apart slowly.

"Rory?" Dean said.

"Yes?" I whispered, looking into his eyes.

Dean hesitated, then said softly, "I love you."

Everything stopped.

I blinked. I couldn't speak.

Dean waited expectantly, and when I still said nothing, his brow furrowed in concern. "Rory?" he prompted.

"Yeah?"

"Did you hear me?"

"Uh huh."

"Well . . . Say something."

"I . . ." I sat up a little. "I . . ."

"Yes?" he encouraged me, searching my face, staring into my eyes.

I turned away, glanced at the steering wheel, the dashboard . . . "I . . . I *love* the car!"

"That's . . . that's it?"

"No. I just . . . I'm surprised. I didn't expect . . . I don't . . ."

"You don't love me." He pulled his arm out from around me and sat up straight.

"No! I—I just have to think for a minute."

"Think about *what?*"

"Well, saying 'I love you' is a really difficult thing."

"Well, I just did it."

"And you did it really well."

"What the hell does *that* mean?"

"I'm sorry—"

Dean exhaled, and his face turned to stone.

"I . . . please," I said, "this totally came as a surprise, I mean, the dinner, and the car, and then the . . . I just need a minute to think about it."

"This is not something that you think about, Rory! This is something that you feel or you don't."

"Please, don't be angry."

"Why? Because I say I love you and . . . and you want to *think* about it? Go home and discuss it with your *mother?* Make one of your *pro/con* lists?" he said angrily.

I stared at my hands. "Not fair," I said.

"I'm sorry. I'm an idiot," he muttered. "I don't even know what I was thinking."

"Dean, please," I pleaded, "it's just not that easy for me. I mean, saying 'I love you' means a lot. Think about it from my point of view. I mean, my mom, and our life . . . I mean, my mom said that she loved my dad and then—"

"You don't get pregnant saying 'I love you,'" he said angrily.

"I know!" I said. "I'm just confused. I need to . . . It's a really big deal."

"Fine. Come on." He started to climb out of the car.

"Please," I said, reaching for him. "Don't be mad."

He backed away from me and held up both hands. "I'll take you home."

"Dean, tonight was amazing," I pleaded, wanting to fix things. "It was perfect. Please. I swear, I just need a minute—"

"Whatever. It doesn't matter," he mumbled. "Let's go." He got out of the car and walked toward the fence, while I sat, stunned, in the front seat of my car.

I took a deep breath. What just happened?

∽

It was a long, silent ride home. When I walked in the door, Mom was on the phone, but she quickly hung up as soon as she saw me, a look of concern on her face. "Rory?"

I looked back at her and told her.

"We just broke up."

∽11

Mom was instantly at my side, and I fell into her arms.

"Tell me what happened."

"We broke up. We just broke up."

"But I don't understand."

"We . . . we went to dinner, and we walked by the bonfire, but it wasn't lit so we went to this junkyard, and we sat in this car and then . . . oh God!"

"What?" she said, alarmed.

"I forgot your meatball in the car."

"Oh, honey, forget it."

"I can't believe I left your meatball in the car."

"Okay. Come on." She led me into the living room and sat me down on the couch. She took off her coat and sat down beside me. "After I told the waiter to wrap it up and everything. And everyone was like, what do you want with one meatball? And I was like, it's a mother-daughter thing. And I'm sure he thought I was nuts, but he was *so* nice and he did it anyway, and then"—I threw up my hands—"I just leave it in the car."

"Okay, forget about the meatball, okay? Just tell me what happened."

"He just broke up with me, okay?" I forced a smile.

Mom looked at me, confused. "But it doesn't make any sense. This is Dean we're talking about. He's *crazy* about you. He calls like twenty-five times a day. Have you seen the cover of his notebook? It's one step away from stalker material."

I couldn't hear this. I got up from the couch. "I have to go to bed."

"But—wait!" Mom followed me to my room. "Just take me through the night, step by step."

"Why?"

"So I can help decipher what happened here?"

"What happened here," I said without looking back at her, "is we broke up. He doesn't want to be my boyfriend anymore. End of story."

"That is so not end of story," Mom said.

I pulled off my coat and threw it on the bed. "Yes, it is!"

"He did not plan an entire romantic evening complete with dinner and a junkyard, which we will get back to later, and then suddenly decide to dump you for absolutely no reason."

I went to my closet and dumped the contents of a cardboard box out on the floor. "How do you know?"

"Because I have read every Nancy Drew mystery ever written. The one about the Amish country twice."

I moved past her and put the box on my bed.

"I know that there is more to this story than what you're telling me," she continued.

I said nothing, but made her move aside so I could reach some books on my desk.

Mom looked at the box, looked at me, and frowned. "What are you doing?"

"I'm getting rid of all this stuff."

"What stuff?"

I dropped the books in the box. "Everything he ever gave me, everything he *touched* . . ." I added a yellow stuffed animal to the box. ". . . everything he *looked* at . . ."

"Okay, honey, will you just calm down for just one sec?"

"He doesn't want to be my boyfriend." I yanked open a drawer and took out some clothes. "Fine."

"Okay, it will be fine, but—" She pulled a black shirt from my hand.

"What?"

"Mine."

"Oh." I went back to my closet, Mom right on my heels. I pulled out a couple of sweaters, hangers and all, and dumped them in the box.

"Is there someone else?"

"No."

"Is he moving?"

"No."

"Is he dying? Did his football team lose a game?"

"What?"

"Hey, it's happened."

I moved the box closer to my closet.

Mom nervously and awkwardly asked the next question. "Did he, um . . . try something?"

I stopped, confused by her question. "What?"

"You know, did he wanna . . ."

"What?"

Mom struggled to get the words out. "Did he want to go . . . faster than you were—"

"God, *no!*"

"Okay, okay—"

"Jeez!"

"I'm sorry! You're just not giving me much to go on here."

I pulled a dress from the closet and stuffed it into the box.

"Honey, that's your fancy dress, that I made for you—"

"That I wore to a dance that I went to with him."

"Oh. Yeah . . ."

I continued filling the box. "That sweater is brand-new," Mom said.

"He saw me in it yesterday and liked it."

"Well, then, he's got good taste."

"He said it brought out the blue in my eyes . . ." I said.

"Well, then he's gay."

I stared at her. "You're not funny and it *goes.*" I shoved it deeper into the box.

"I'm a little funny, and if you throw away everything that Dean ever saw you wear, you'll be walking around in a towel."

I added my stuffed chicken to the pile.

"Colonel Clucker?" Mom picked up the big fat bird and held it up in the air. "Are you serious? He's been with you since you were four."

"The first time Dean came over, he picked it up!" I stated.

"Yeah, well, that's not the Colonel's fault. He was just sitting there minding his own business when a guy comes in and picks him up. What's a stuffed bird to do?" she asked, trying to lighten my mood.

"I don't want to joke about this!" I said forcefully. "Not now." I pulled off my bracelet and threw it into the box, then put Colonel Clucker on top. I handed the box to Mom. "Here. Take this. I don't want to look at it anymore."

"Okay," Mom said in a sad voice. "I'll, uh, put it away."

"No! Take it out of the house! Throw it in a Dumpster. *Burn* it. I don't care. Just . . ." I sank down on my bed. "I want it *gone*."

Mom put the box on the end of my bed, and sat down in front of me.

"You know, honey, someday, when all this is all in the past, you might be sorry you don't have those things anymore—"

"I don't care."

"But, Rory—"

"I don't *care!*"

"Okay. Fine. It's gone."

"Thank you." I stared at my lap.

"So I'll take care of it, and you go to bed. Get some rest. Maybe you'll feel more like talking in the morning."

"Okay."

"Ohh, honey. Good night." She leaned over and kissed me, then picked up the box and headed for the door.

"Mom?"

"Yeah?"

"Far, far away from the house. Okay?"

"Hey, it sleeps with the fishes."

"Thank you."

She winked at me, and closed the door behind her.
I turned out the lights and crawled under the covers.

"Mom?"

"Mmmm."

"Mom. Get up!" I shook her awake.

"Rory? What's the matter?" Mom mumbled through the covers.

"Nothing. I just want to get started."

I went to her window and pulled the shade up, letting the morning sunlight into her room. "I made a list of all the things that we always say we're going to do on weekends, but then when the weekend comes around, you say they're too boring to actually do on a weekend day, so you say we'll do them during the week which, of course, we never do."

Mom pulled her furry purple alarm clock close to her face and tried to read the time.

"So," I continued, "I think we should get them all out of the way today, once and for all. And to make it interesting, we could come up with, like, a reward system so once we're done with everything on the list, we can get manicures."

I opened her closet and dug out some clothes for her. Mom rubbed her eyes and tried to focus on the time again.

"*Or,*" I continued, suddenly excited, "we can go to that Swiss place for fondue for dinner. Or we can stuff our purses with Sour Patch Kids and Milk Duds and go see the Stars Hollow Elementary School production of *Who's Afraid of Virginia Woolf?*" I sat on her bed and smiled into her sleepy face.

Mom held up her clock in disbelief. "It's six o'clock."

"I know."

"On Saturday morning."

"That's right."

"Ah! It's six o'clock on Saturday morning," she repeated.

"Do you want to wear Docs or sneakers?"

"I *want* to wear . . . *slippers*."

I gave her my most cheerful smile. "Up, please."

"Rory, my heart, it's Saturday. The day of rest."

"Sunday is the day of rest."

"No, Saturday is the day of pre-rest."

"Pre-rest?"

"So that way, when you actually get to Sunday, you're rested enough to . . . enjoy your rest."

"That makes absolutely no sense."

She waved the clock and protested, "That's because it's six o'clock on Saturday morning!"

I smiled—pulled the covers off her bed.

"Aw, jeez!"

"Up, please!"

"Hey, you rhymed."

"I'll meet you downstairs."

I ran downstairs while Mom got ready. A short while later she emerged, and found me sitting at the kitchen table, working on my list.

"Hel-lo," Mom said in a cheerful voice. After a moment she asked, "Did you rearrange the furniture?"

"Yes," I said proudly. I was feeling very efficient.

"Oh, good. 'Cause for a moment there I thought we were having a problem with decorator elves and I was going to have to call the exterminator and tent the place . . . but it was just you. Great.

She paused for a moment, then continued. "So, any particular reason why you suddenly felt the need to move large pieces of furniture around first thing in the morning?"

"I was up. It was there." I smiled and went back to my list.

"Okay. Good thought process. Now, I noticed you didn't move the TV, though."

"It was too heavy."

"Right, okay. I like this. Yeah. This is good. Now, of course, when the sofa actually faced the TV, it made it a little easier to watch, but you know, this is good too. It'll be like, um, you know, like radio."

"Are you ready to go?"

"Yeah, I am. Just one quick sec." Mom sat down next to me. "Um, why don't you . . . Would you put the pen down?"

"I'm finishing the list."

"Yes, I see. And as much as I love your lists, let's just, ah"—she gently pulled the pen from my fingers—"finish this particular one later, okay?"

"Okay." I sat up and looked at her.

"Honey, I'm concerned about you," she began. "I wish you'd talk to me."

"I don't really want to deal with it right now. I can't really deal with it now."

"I know. But listen. I've had my heart broken before. It's really hard. It's hard for everybody. So, can I give you a little advice?"

"Okay."

"I think what you really need to do today is wallow."

"Wallow?"

"Get back in your pajamas, go to bed, eat nothing

but gallons of ice cream and tons of pizza, don't take a shower or shave your legs or put on any sort of makeup *at all*, sit in the dark, watch really sad movies, and have a good long cry, and just *wallow*. You need to wallow."

"No," I said quickly.

"Rory, your first love is intense. Your first breakup, even more intense. Shoving this away and ignoring it while you make lists isn't going to help."

"I don't want to wallow."

"Try it for one day."

"No."

"One day. One day of pizza and pajamas, I'll rent *Love Story* and *The Champ*, *An Affair to Remember*, *Ishtar* —"

"I don't want to be that kind of girl."

"The kind of girl who watches *Ishtar*?"

"The kind of girl who just falls apart because she doesn't have a boyfriend."

"That description hardly applies to you."

"Well, it will if I wallow."

"Not true."

"So, I used to have a boyfriend and now I don't." I gathered up my notebook and pens and my empty glass and stood up. "Okay. That's the way it is. I mean, sitting in the dark eating junk food and not shaving my legs is not going to change that. Is it?" I dumped my things on the counter and started absent-mindedly washing my glass.

"No, but—"

"So, I don't even want to go there. I have things to do. I have school and Harvard to think on."

"Honey, Harvard is like three years away."

"But now is the time that I should be preparing for it." I put my glass in the sink and turned to face her. "I mean, Harvard is hard to get into. And I don't know why I even spend my time thinking about anything else."

"Because you have a pulse and are not the president of the audiovisual club," Mom replied.

"I'm sixteen. I have the rest of my life to have a boyfriend. I should be keeping my eye on the prize right now."

"I admire your attitude."

"Thank you."

"Should we rent *Old Yeller* too, or is that just a guys' crying movie?"

"You are not listening to me."

"I am listening to you. I just don't agree with you."

"I don't want to wallow," I said emphatically. "And you can't make me."

"Okay, fine."

"Thank you." I got my paper and pen off the counter and sat back down at the table.

"So, that must be the list."

"Yes, it is."

"May I see it, please?"

I handed her the sheet and she scanned it. "We do *not* need a garden hose."

"We don't have one."

"We don't have a garden either."

"Well, maybe with a hose we can grow one."

"Okay. Can I see the pen."

"Why?"

"Small adjustment, small adjustment." She took my pen, then wrote something at the bottom, and slowly handed the paper back to me.

She'd written one tiny word. In all caps.

WALLOW.

"*Mom . . .*"

"What? It's on your list. Don't you have to do it if it's on your list?"

"I am *not* going to wallow," I said, as I crossed it off.

"But I put it *after* going to the recycling center!" she said.

I just looked at her and she gave in.

"Fine. Forget it. I give. I need coffee. Let's go."

We put on our coats and headed out the door for Luke's.

Stars Hollow was bustling with townspeople cleaning up after the Firelight Festival.

Mom looked around in disbelief. "What are all these people doing up? It's Saturday morning!"

"Some people like getting up early," I pointed out.

"You lie."

"They do it voluntarily."

"Really?"

"Every day."

"Jump back!"

"Excuse me?"

"Kevin Bacon. *Footloose*. Reaction to the no-dancing rule in town as revealed to him by Chris Penn, brother to Sean, sage to all."

"I should've known."

"Yes, you should've. I don't know what they teach you in that damn school."

Suddenly I stopped in the middle of the sidewalk.

"What?"

"I can't go that way."

"Why? We're going to Luke's."

"No."

"You pull me out of bed at six in the morning and then you say no to Luke's? Don't you realize how dangerous that is?"

"I can't go that way."

"Reason, please."

"Because we'd have to go past Doose's Market."

"So?"

"So . . . we might run into . . ."

"Oh."

"Yes."

"Right. You don't know if he's working?"

"I don't remember. His weekend schedule changes a lot."

"Okay, well, we'll just take the long way."

"No."

"Why?"

"We'd have to go by the school."

"There's no school today."

"No, but on the days that he doesn't work, he plays football at the school with some of his friends."

"What time?"

"It varies."

"Okay. Well, we'll just go down Peach and circle around . . . You're shaking your head, why?"

"Dean lives on Peach."

Mom began to look desperate. "Okay, Rory, honey, love of my life, you realize you've completely cut us off from Luke's where the happy coffee is."

"I'm sorry."

"No, no, it's okay, it's okay." Mom slipped her arm

through mine and looked around. "We'll just . . . we'll figure something out."

Soon we were weaving our way down an alley, through piles of garbage, past a street cat eating out of an old can, and heading toward the back of Luke's Diner.

"Sorry," I said.

"No, this is good!" Mom replied. "It's like *G.I. Jane*, but we get to keep our hair."

"I just couldn't—"

"Honey, say no more. Think of this as an *adventure*. Two girls battling the elements. Desperate for survival."

"Or coffee."

"Same thing."

"You know, I bet you can tell a lot about people by their garbage," I said as we continued on.

"Yeah?"

"Think about it. Trash is discarded aspects of people's lives. It talks about their eating habits, what they read, do they go to concerts, are they responsible, do they pay their bills on time . . ."

Mom turned to face me. She grabbed my hands, a little concerned. "You know, honey, trash doesn't actually talk at all unless it's on *Sesame Street*."

"I'm just trying to make a point."

"That going through people's garbage is interesting."

"And educational."

"And stinky. And a little nuts."

"There's nothing nuts about wanting to know more about human nature. Curiosity is how we grow." I started to look through a pile of old clothes.

Mom wrinkled her nose and pulled me away." "We need to get you out of this alley."

⌒∽

Luke's was incredibly packed, and although we eat there almost every morning, we knew no one.

"Who *are* all these people?" Mom said, completely stunned by what she was seeing.

"This is the six A.M. crowd."

"I officially recognize nobody in this place."

"Hey," said a voice from behind us. Mom whirled around and came face to face with Luke's old girlfriend, Rachel. With her long, curly, honey-blond hair pulled back, her big brown eyes bright and rested, her skin glowing, she looked wide awake—and beautiful.

"Oh, hi!" Mom said, with her best forced smile.

Rachel held up two huge mugs in one hand and a pot of coffee in the other. "Coffee while you wait?"

"Ah. Bless you!" Mom said.

We gratefully took the mugs.

"So, Luke put you to work, huh?" Mom said.

Rachel filled our mugs. "Yeah, well, I figured if I'm going to be hanging around here for a while, the least I can do is help out."

"So, you're—gonna be—hanging around? For a while? Here?" Mom said, a little surprised.

"Yeah." Rachel smiled. "I think so."

"Oh well." Mom nodded. "That's nice."

"Yeah." Rachel nodded.

"So, where is Luke?" I asked.

"Well, we were up kind of late last night," Rachel said, "so I let him sleep in."

"Sleep in? Luke?" Mom said with a laugh.

"Believe me, it wasn't easy to get him to agree to it, but in the end, a little sweet talk, a couple Excedrin PMs, he finally caved in," Rachel said. Then she moved on to the other customers.

We sat down at the table next to the front window. Someone a few seats away laughed. A wave of paranoia washed over me and I looked around. "I feel like everyone's looking at me."

"Well, yeah," Mom said without missing a beat. "'Cause you've got a banana peel stuck to your foot."

"I do?" I looked under the table at my shoe.

"I'm kidding! Nobody's staring at you."

I started pulling my coat off and stopped suddenly, one arm still in the jacket. I looked around again. "They *know*."

"They don't know."

"It's probably all around town by now."

"Honey, it happened last night. It's six in the morning!" Mom reassured me.

"It's all over town." I pulled my coat the rest of the way off and put it in my lap. "Everyone knows I've been *dumped*."

"Do you want to go home?" Mom said as she laid her hand on mine.

"No. We have a list!" I said resolutely.

Mom quickly supported me. "Okay. Great. I'm going to order us something. Any preferences? Eggs? French toast? Key to the Dumpster?"

"I don't care."

"I'll be right back." Mom headed to the counter, passing the front door just as Miss Patty entered. "Lorelai," she said. "What a nice surprise so early in the morning? So . . . how's things?"

They chatted for a few moments, then Mom continued to the counter toward Luke, who had just come downstairs.

Kirk came up to my table and said bluntly, "I never liked him. I don't know exactly what it was. Something about the shape of his forehead, or his height, or the floppy hairstyle. Actually, yes. On reflection, I think it was the floppy hairstyle."

I was stunned. Mom suddenly appeared, saving me. "Hey. Good morning, Kirk."

"Lorelai." Kirk turned. "I want to express my apologies for not voicing my concerns about that floppy-haired *jerk* earlier, because if I had—"

"Don't! You know what? You need to leave now!" Mom quickly said.

"I cannot go until you accept my apology," Kirk continued.

"I accept your apology," Mom said.

"All right." He started to walk away, then turned back to assure us, "It will not happen again."

Mom slid into her seat. "Honey, are you sure you don't want to—"

"Do not say *wallow*," I warned.

"*Sw-w-w-wallow* your coffee before you eat?"

"I am fine," I insisted with a smile.

"But if you saw the look on your face . . ."

"It's the same look you had on your face when you broke up with Max. Did wallowing help you get over him?"

"I am not saying wallowing will get you over Dean," Mom conceded. "It's part of the process. It's the mourning period. It's a step. An *important* step. But the only thing that will get you over somebody is time."

"How much time did it take you to get over Max?"

"Oh, well, I'm not sure exactly."

"Approximately."

"I didn't clock it."

"Ballpark figure," I pressed.

"A while."

"Be vaguer."

"Rory, come on."

"More coffee?" Luke interrupted as he filled our cups without waiting for an answer. Then he pointed at me and almost smiled. "The pancakes are coming right up. Anything else I can get you?"

"No, thanks."

"Hey!" he said suddenly. "I've got some strawberries back there. You like strawberries, right?"

I blinked. Luke was abnormally cheerful. "Yeah, I like strawberries, but—"

"I'm getting you strawberries." He pointed at me and grinned as he walked away.

I sighed and looked at Mom. "You told him, didn't you."

"No! Miss Patty did."

I wasn't sure I believed her.

"If you tell Miss Patty, everybody in town is going to know," I stated.

"Honey, people have their own lives and their own problems. I hardly think that you breaking up with Dean is the main thing on their minds." Mom took a sip of her coffee and glanced out the window, then nearly chocked. Her hand flew to her mouth. "Oh my God!"

"What?" I followed her gaze.

Luke had Dean in a headlock in the middle of the street and Dean was struggling to get loose.

"Oh my God." I was completely stunned. How was this happening?

Mom grabbed her purse and coat and was halfway

out the door before I could react. I got my things and ran after her.

"Hey! Hey! Cut it out! Break it up!" Mom said, finally separating them.

"What do you think you're doing?" she yelled at Luke.

"He started it!" Luke said, trying to catch his breath.

"By doing what?"

"He was coming in!" As if that explained it all.

"Are you a lunatic? He's sixteen!"

"Well, what was I supposed to do?" he snapped.

"Well, stand in the middle of the street and have a slap fight, of course." She grabbed him by the arm and dragged him toward the entrance to the diner. "C'mere!"

I turned back to Dean.

He just stood there in the middle of the street, breathing hard.

"You okay?" I asked.

"I'm fine," he muttered. He wouldn't even look at me.

"Oh, good!" I said. "I don't know what got into Luke. He's usually so—"

Dean shoved past me. "I have to go."

"Oh. Sure. Bye."

He walked away, passing Luke. Luke went after him again and Dean put up his hands defensively, backing away.

"Get inside now!" Mom demanded, pulling Luke by the shoulder.

"But—"

"*Inside! Now!*" she commanded.

"He started it," Luke pouted as he headed back into the diner.

I stood in the middle of the street and watched Dean walk away.

He never looked back.

✑12

I felt a tug on my jacket.

Mom was at my side. "Hey."

"Hey."

"So . . . what's first on the list?" she said, smiling brightly.

"What?"

"The list. We've got a lot of things to get done today, missy. Otherwise I'm going to be dragging your butt out of bed at six again tomorrow morning. So, where do we start?"

"Well, um . . ." My hands trembled a little as I dug the list out of my pocket and unfolded it. "We need . . . a soap dish for the kitchen."

"Ah! A kitchen soap dish!" Mom exclaimed. "Quite decadent, but what the hell . . ." She put her arm through mine and led me down the street. "Let's go."

What can I tell you? We ended up having fun. Mom

made it fun. By the time we came home, the diner incident was almost forgotten.

"Well, that was a very successful outing for us," I said cheerfully as I set down my shopping bags. "We got everything on the list except the brown extension cord."

"Which will be in on Tuesday."

"So, I think that qualifies as a check, too."

"Are you happy?"

"I appreciate a job well done. Yes."

Mom dug into the grocery bags. "I can't wait to try the toaster pizza. It looks so gross. Which is usually the mark of great junk food."

"Beef a Roni," I pointed out.

" 'Nuff said."

"I'm going to go plug in my new wall air freshener," I told Mom. "Give me five minutes and then come sniff my room."

She held up the two pizza boxes. "Cheese or pepperoni?"

"Whatever."

"Both. Good choice."

I closed my door to quicken the effect of the air freshener and I tried it out on different outlets, then chose the one near the door.

I went back out to Mom and the pizzas but stopped when I heard Mom out on the back porch, talking to Babette.

"But I can help!" Babette was saying. "I can tell her how you have to go through a lot of bad relationships to get to that really good one. I can tell her about all the really horrible men I've known in my day. Really truly awful men."

"Really, Babette—"

"I was pushed out of a moving car once."

"Well, that's a peppy little anecdote," Mom said. "I want you to tell her all of that. Just not right now."

"Is she really bad?"

"She'll be fine. Really."

I retreated back to my room, closed the door, and fell back on my bed, looking at my wrist where Dean's bracelet used to be.

I curled up on my side and felt myself starting to cry. Determined not to let this overcome me, I sat up and pulled my backpack up to me. With a renewed sense of determination, I opened it up and pulled out some homework. A crumpled piece of paper fell out from the pile and I unfolded a computer-printed flyer with a fancy color border.

It was Madeline's party invitation. I'd forgotten all about it because I never intended to go in the first place.

I got up from the bed and walked back into the kitchen.

"Look." I held out the flyer.

Mom took it from me. "Madeline's having a party tonight," she read.

I nodded and stated, "*I'm* going to go."

"*You're* going to a *Chilton* party?"

"Yes, I am."

It was a little surprising considering you could never say the word "Madeline" without "Paris" and "Louise" attached to it. They were always together.

"Honey, why don't you just stay home and read *The Bell Jar*? Same effect." She opened up the pizza boxes and put a couple in the toaster.

"Hey, I'm going to be going to school there for the next two and a half years. It wouldn't kill me to be social. Right? What's wrong with that?" I reasoned.

"Nothing."

"Okay, then. It's settled." I opened up the cabinet to grab the Parmesan cheese.

Mom cleared her throat. "Um, can I make a suggestion?"

"Go ahead."

"Why don't you see if Lane can go with you? You know, that way if the socializing doesn't turn out how you planned, you've got a friendly face around."

"Okay. Good idea. Thank you."

"You're welcome."

"Can I take the car?"

"Yes."

"Can I borrow something to wear?"

"Yes."

"Are you going to give in to anything I say 'cause you feel sorry for me?" I said with a smile.

"Yes!"

"I'll make a list."

I was feeling okay again. I ran to call Lane.

∽

Lane had on a cute red sweater, short jean skirt, black tights and heels when she came over that night. She looked great. I was wearing a pretty flowered dress. We had fun putting the finishing touches on our outfits.

"Am I all twisted back here?" I asked her.

She checked the back of my dress. "A little. Here." As she straightened the back of my dress, she suddenly got very quiet. "So . . . how are you?"

We hadn't really talked about things. "I'm . . . fine."

"How are you really?"

I shrugged and turned around with my automatic smile. "Life goes on, right?"

"You know, I saw Dean today—I wasn't sure if I should tell you."

"Why not?"

"I mean, I wasn't sure you'd want to know."

"No, that's fine." I tried to sound casual as I asked, "What did he say?"

"Nothing. He crossed the street as soon as I saw him."

"Oh." I walked toward my bed, staring down at my hands.

Lane followed me and we sat down on my bed. "But if it's any consolation, he looked really sad."

"I don't want him to be sad." I picked up a book from the pile on my bed and stuffed it into my purse.

"Rory, are you sure you want to go out tonight?" Lane asked softly.

"Why does everyone keep asking me that?"

"Because you just broke up. I mean, I'd be perfectly fine to just hang out here and listen to music. Talk. Not talk. Whatever."

"No. I am not hanging out!" I stood up. "We are going to this party. It's going to be *great*. I don't want to dwell on this, and that's final."

"Don't argue with her or you'll find yourself the proud owner of three garden weasels," Mom said as she came into the room, carrying a necklace.

"Mom . . ." I tried to defend my purchase from earlier in the day.

"Three. 'Cause one's just not enough. Turn around."

"Why?"

"Fourteen hours of labor, that's why."

"Fine."

I turned around in front of the mirror as she put the necklace on me.

"What's this?" I asked.

"I thought it would go with your dress and it does."

It was perfect. "Pretty."

"Yeah. It's really pretty. Now, here's the cell phone, and some mad money. If for any reason you think you won't be home before twelve, you call me."

"Oh, we'll be back by twelve," Lane said.

"Hi. Call me," Mom said.

"Sorry," Lane replied.

I closed my makeup case, then froze when I saw the small yellow box wedged up against my mirror.

"Rory?" Mom asked in concern.

"The cornstarch."

"What?"

"The cornstarch that . . . the first time Dean kissed me . . ."

The first time Dean kissed me, I'd been in Doose's Market, pretending to shop for cornstarch, but when he kissed me, I'd been so startled, I ran out of the store without paying for it.

I'd kept it on my dressing table ever since, a memento of my first kiss.

"I forgot to put it in with the other things," I said. "I'll just throw it out."

"Hey!" Mom grabbed the box out of my hand. "Why don't you let me do that? You guys get going."

"Okay." We kissed each other goodbye.

"Bye! Have fun!" she called after us. "Be good. Ooh! Make sure you look in somebody's sock drawers. Rich people have hilarious sock drawers."

Lane and I laughed as we grabbed our coats and headed out into the night.

∾

Lane was highly impressed by Madeline's house. It was like the mansion in *Citizen Kane*, only this one was filled with teenagers and the fine musical tunes of Beck, Billy Bragg and Elvis Costello. The ballroom was her favorite, and it really was stunning with its marble columns, geometrically patterned floors, and a huge domed ceiling made of gold glass.

"Wow!" Lane said. "This is unbelievable. My wedding won't be this big."

"Yeah." I giggled.

"This is amazing. People live here?"

"This is Madeline's house." I explained.

"Is this what your grandparents' house looks like?

"No. I mean, it's big but it's not this Hearst Castle-y."

"I mean, there should be like a map, or a tour guide, or Robin Leach here or something," Lane said.

"Hey, Lane?" I said.

"Yeah?"

"Thanks for coming with me."

"Any time." Then she spotted something. "Oh, my God, there's a pool table!"

"And a DJ."

"It's like teenage Sodom and Gomorrah."

Suddenly Madeline cut a path through the crowd, followed predictably by Louise and Paris. "You came!" Madeline squealed.

"Who's watching the farm?" Louise asked dryly.

I ignored her. "Madeline, your house is beautiful."

"Thanks. It's my stepfather's."

"So . . . where is he?" Louise questioned.

"My stepfather?" Madeline shook her head. "He's in Japan. I told you."

"Not your stepfather." Louise grinned at me. "Prince Charming."

I looked down and tried to smile. "He didn't come."

"Why?"

"Um, his white horse was in the shop."

"You guys didn't break up, did you?" Louise asked.

Beside me, Lane quickly diverted the conversation. "Hi, I'm Lane."

Louise looked her up and down. "As in, walk down a . . . ?"

"Yes. Exactly."

"Hi. I'm Madeline," our host said cheerfully.

Just then a couple of guys came over and draped themselves over Madeline and Louise.

"So, when does the tour of the pool house start?" one of them said.

Madeline shook her head. "You've seen the pool house before."

"Yes, but they've never seen it at night. Right?" he replied.

Madeline looked clueless. "But —"

"Madeline," Louise interrupted. "You are not confused. Think. Process. Focus."

Lane and I exchanged a look.

And then suddenly Madeline got it. "Ohhhh." She grinned at us. "Bye."

"Later, Paris," Louise cooed.

"No glove, no love," Paris responded as she checked her watch.

"Lovely," Louise replied as they walked away.

"So," Paris said as we followed her through the

crowd. "I didn't think you were that much of a party girl."

I shrugged. "I'm not usually. I just thought I'd come by and check it out."

"Well, it's the same exact people we see every single day at school except now we get to see them dance. So, where is your boyfriend?"

"We, um . . . we broke up," I admitted.

"Oh." For a second, a glimmer of humanity flashed in Paris's face as she picked at something on the table. "Well, at least you had a boyfriend for a while."

"So, do you know which way might lead to the soda?" I asked, trying to steer the conversation in a different direction.

Paris's ice-cold mask came back up and she led us through the crowd. "Keep up, because I'm not turning around."

"Wow," Lane whispered behind me. "You didn't exaggerate."

"Paris needs no embellishment," I whispered back.

Soon we arrived at this giant mountain of bottles and cans on ice. Lane looked at all the labels. "All this soda is French!"

"Madeline's mother has a French fetish," Paris explained. "She's obsessed with all things French. French wine, French food, French water, French cellulite products . . ."

Then I heard someone say, "Look, why won't you answer me?" It was Tristin, with Summer, his latest girlfriend.

"Because you didn't say please," Summer responded.

"Summer . . ."

"Can we do this later? There's a party going on," Summer said with a pout.

"Just tell me what you were doing locked in the bathroom with Austin!" Tristin demanded.

Summer flipped her long brown hair over her shoulder and looked bored. "Nothing."

"Nothing."

"Yep."

"Nope."

"Well, why don't you tell me what I was doing since you seem to know everything."

"Hey, you are my girlfriend!"

"Ooh, now he's a caveman," she taunted. "What are you going to do," she said loudly, "knock me on the head with your club and drag me back to your Porsche?" She walked off.

Tristin caught her by the arm. "Summer, please . . ."

She turned and snapped her finger. "Ooh, good song." And she danced off into a crowd of waiting guys.

Tristin turned and noticed me watching. He looked totally humiliated and quickly disappeared into the crowd.

"I just love that Summer, don't you?" Paris said flippantly. She sighed and glanced at her watch again. "Nine forty-five."

"Why do you keep checking your watch?" I asked.

"My mom said I had to stay until ten thirty." She walked to the entrance to the ballroom and leaned against the doorway, staring at the dancing crowd.

I followed her while Lane stayed behind, fascinated by the French beverages.

"Why would she care?" I asked.

"She thinks I'm not enough of a people person. Shocking, huh?"

"I'm floored."

"Yeah, well, I doubt highly that Madame Curie was voted most likely to dress like Jennifer Lopez."

"You want to be a scientist?"

"Cancer research."

"Cool."

"Yeah."

Lane had rejoined us and suddenly ducked her head. "Oh no," she groaned.

"What?"

"It just figures that the one Korean boy at the party has his Korean girl radar turned on," she said.

I looked up and saw this really cute Korean boy coming toward us. I'd seen him around Chilton, but I didn't know his name.

"Hi," he said to Lane with a nice smile. "I'm Henry."

"I'm Lane. This is Rory and Paris."

"We've met," Paris muttered.

"Hi, Paris," he said politely. Then he glanced back at Lane. "So, would you like to dance?"

"Oh, well . . . we're kind of talking here."

"Oh. Yeah. But I mean one dance?" Again, with the charming smile. "You can put the conversation on hold for one dance, right? Unless this is a Mideast peace talk kind of conversation."

Lane gave in. "One dance."

"A short one. No crazy dance mixes," Henry promised.

"Okay."

"Thank you."

Lane pulled off her coat and handed it to me. "If I'm not back in one dance," she whispered, "you are coming down with a really bad case of anything that means we have to go home."

"Ooh, is it warm in here, or is it just me?" I said.

"Thank you."

Paris watched Lane and Henry as they walked off to the dance floor. "Unbelievable. She's here five minutes, she has a date. I've been going to this school nine years, and I'm the French soda monitor." She walked away, and I decided to let her enjoy her misery in peace.

I looked back at Lane. She and Henry were really getting into it. He was a great dancer, almost as good as she was and she didn't look too miserable, so I decided to see the rest of the house.

As I wandered around, I spotted Tristin leaning against a wall watching Summer dance with another guy. He looked absolutely miserable.

Billy Bragg's "From Red to Blue" started playing and people started slow-dancing to the song. I realized it was probably time to check in on Lane, so I headed back to the ballroom.

I spotted her slow-dancing with Henry like they'd known each other for years. I tapped her on the shoulder and whispered, "Am I sick yet?"

Lane smiled. "Not yet. It actually might just be allergies."

"Keep me posted," I whispered back.

I smiled at her and walked away.

Suddenly Paris rushed up to me, completely panicked. "My watch stopped!" she said frantically. "What time is it?"

I glanced at my watch. "It's ten thirty-five."

"Yes! Bye!" And she bolted for the door.

I wandered into a relatively quiet side room and sat down in a cozy, overstuffed chair, and pulled the ever-present book out of my purse.

As I started to read, Summer stormed in, Tristin trailing her.

"Tristin, stop it."

"You're making me chase you around the whole party," he complained.

"I'm just trying to have fun."

"You won't talk to me, you won't dance with me, why the hell did you even come with me?"

"Stop yelling."

"Summer, please, can't we just go?"

"No!"

"*Please*."

By now, a small crowd had gathered.

"No! I'm sick of fighting with you. I'm sick of hearing twenty times a day 'you're my girlfriend.'"

Tristin suddenly realized the crowd had gathered and lowered his voice. "Can we possibly do this somewhere where a room full of people aren't staring at us?'"

"I think we should break up," she said as she munched on a pretzel.

"Okay, I *really* want to go outside and talk about this—"

"Then go," Summer said indifferently. "Bye!" And she walked back to the party.

"Summer, come on!" Tristin called after her.

But she was gone.

Some of the people standing around snickered.

In spite of our history, I felt sorry for him.

He saw me watching again. I averted my eyes and he walked out of the room, almost knocking Lane over as she came in. She was visibly upset. "I have a major problem."

"What?" I said.

"Henry, the guy I've been dancing with?"

"Yes?"

"Okay." She began to pace back and forth in front of me. "So he's really good in school, he's going to be a doctor, pediatrician to be exact, his parents are extremely involved in their local church. He himself helps out with Sunday school. He speaks Korean fluently, he respects his parents, and he's also really cute, very funny, and surprisingly interesting."

"Lane, I'm sorry, but I am totally failing to see the problem here."

"I'm falling for a guy my parents would approve of! They would *love* him! They'd go crazy! There'd be dancing in the Kim house! Dancing!" she said, bordering on hysterical.

"Really?"

"Followed by a lot of praying, but initially, there'd be dancing," she said, wringing her hands. "This is horrible. It can't happen. I have to stop it. We need to go."

"But—"

"No, now!" She pulled my arm to get me up. "You need to grab your stuff! We gotta go!"

"Whatever you say." I quickly grabbed my book and purse and got up.

We headed for the exit, just as Henry came around the corner. "Hey," he said.

Lane froze. "Henry. Hi."

He turned to me. "Sorry I've been monopolizing Lane all night." And again, champion smile.

"Oh, that's okay. I've had her for fifteen years. I'm actually a little sick of her."

"Thank you," Lane muttered.

"You're welcome." I glanced at Lane. "We should go."

Henry looked surprised. "You're going?"

"Yeah, I have to go home. I have a very strict mother."

Henry winced. "Oh, wow. Sorry about that." He

turned to Lane. "You couldn't even stay for one more dance, huh?"

I shook my head, making it seem like it was all my fault. "I don't think—"

"Yes!" Lane interrupted.

"Excuse me?"

"One dance would be fine," she said.

Henry's eyes lit up "Great."

"But—"

Henry pulled Lane back to the dance floor. "I'll be back!" she called happily over her shoulder.

I guess it was back to the wandering for me.

Luckily Madeline's house was like a hotel; each new hall seemed to lead to dozens more rooms. I went into what I hoped was an empty one and heard the plunking of piano notes. Tristin was sitting at the grand piano sadly hitting the keys.

"Oh. Sorry," I said.

"No problem."

"I'm . . . sorry."

"About what?"

"About you and Summer."

He shook his head and looked down at the keys. "I don't want to talk about Summer."

"Okay." I took a step forward. "So, how did you do on the biology test?"

"What?"

"The test. It was hard, wasn't it?"

"Yeah," he said, confused. "It was hard."

"I got a B plus." I laid my bag on the top of the piano.

"What are you doing?" he asked.

"I'm talking about the test."

"Why?"

"Because you didn't want to talk about Summer."

"I don't."

"Okay. So I moved to biology. Sorry. Did you want to talk about Spanish?"

Tristin thought I was mocking him. "You just loved it, didn't you?"

"Loved what?"

"Seeing me nailed like that. Must've been a great moment."

"Not really."

"Please, you loved it. She loved it. Everybody loved it."

I'd never heard him sound so . . . real. Like a normal person, with normal feelings. "I did not love it," I said as I sat down beside him on the piano bench.

"I really liked her too," he said softly.

"Yeah. I know."

"So," he said, "where's your *boyfriend* tonight?" giving the word "boyfriend" a slightly sarcastic twist.

I don't know why, but I told him the truth. "He's . . . not my boyfriend anymore."

He was surprised. "Why not?"

"He didn't want to be."

"*Idiot.*"

"So is Summer," I replied.

He'd stopped playing altogether now and just sat staring into space. "You think you'll get back together?" he asked me.

I stared down at my hands. "He seemed pretty set in his decision."

Tristin turned to me. "When did it happen?" he asked quietly.

"Yesterday."

"Wow."

I nodded. "It was our three-month anniversary."

"That sucks."

"Yeah. It does suck. You think you guys will . . ."

"No. No. No, no, no, no, no," he said, vigorously shaking his head.

"So . . . no?" I said.

He smiled. "No."

We sat in silence for a moment, lost in our own thoughts.

"Hey," he said at last. "I'm sorry I gave you such a hard time for a while."

"Oh. That's okay."

"It is?"

"Well, no." I smiled at him. "But you're sad."

"Yeah. Well, I am sorry."

"I accept your apology."

"You're welcome."

We both got quiet for a moment. "Oh man," he said, "this is a great party, huh?"

"Yeah, not bad. It gave me a chance to catch up on my reading."

He looked at me. "You are very odd, you know that?"

"Thank you."

"You're welcome."

We looked at each other, united by our pain.

He leaned forward and kissed me.

And for a small quiet moment, I kissed him back.

Then I jerked away, holding back tears.

"I'm sorry," Tristin mumbled, embarrassed. "What did I do? Did I bite your lip or something?"

I jumped up. "No. It's not you. I—I have to go."

I ran out the door and back into the party, weaving my way through the crowd, searching for Lane, trying not to cry in front of all my Chilton classmates.

At last I spotted her. "We have to go," I said urgently.

"Rory? Are you okay?" Lane asked, concerned.

I felt the tears starting to roll down my face, so I turned and ran toward the door.

Behind me, I heard Lane tell Henry, "I have to go."

"Wait, can I get your number?" Henry called after her.

"Last name's Kim. We're the only ones in Stars Hollow!" she called back as she ran to catch up to me.

We drove back and Lane came into the empty house with me, refusing to leave until Mom returned. I reassured her I'd be fine and that my mom couldn't be far since we had her car. She eventually left, mostly because it was getting close to her curfew and her mom was probably already waiting for her.

I went to my room and tried to read but I couldn't concentrate. I finally put on my pajamas and wandered into the kitchen. There was a large bucket of Ben & Jerry's ice cream in the freezer so I took it out and went to the living room, curling up on the couch.

Mom got home a few minutes later and walked into the living room with a smile on her face that disappeared the second she saw mine.

"I'm ready to wallow now," I told her as the tears I had been holding back flowed down my face.

Mom was beside me right away, kissing away my hurt. Without a word, she removed the ice cream bucket from my hands, then put a pillow in her lap and patted it. I laid my head on the pillow and began to weep.

With one hand Mom stroked my hair, and with the other she dialed the cordless phone.

"Hey, Joe, it's Lorelai," she whispered over the soft sounds of my crying. "I need a large pizza with everything . . ."

ೲ13

Wallowing did help make the breakup a little easier, and maybe if I had wallowed before Madeline's party, the whole Tristin kiss thing wouldn't have happened, but it did. And, as fate would have it, we were assigned to the same study group that following Monday at school.

It was a little uncomfortable during the meeting but right after we talked about it and agreed it had been a bad night for both of us. I suggested that maybe he needed to start looking at different types of girls and even convinced him to ask Paris out on a date. That didn't end as well as I had hoped, and even triggered Paris hating me again. It was too bad, because Paris and I had just gotten to the point where outsiders might have considered us friends.

School was a nice distraction, but soon I realized how much of my life was affected by my breakup with Dean. For instance, I could no longer go into Doose's

Market on Wednesdays for fear I would run into him. And people started treating me like a porcelain doll when it came to Dean, avoiding any reference to him at all. It started to make me crabby.

Lane and I got into the biggest fight of our lives when I walked in on her and Dean studying. She had been too afraid of reminding me of the breakup to tell me they had been assigned as science study partners.

And that led to an even bigger fight with my mom when I found out she, too, had been withholding information from me, like the very important fact she and Max had discussed getting back together, because she didn't want to brag about her potentially blossoming love life when mine had just died.

I just got fed up and had to get away so I took a cab to my grandparents' house. My grandmother had just finished setting up a room for me there and it just seemed like a safe place to go. I guess I should have told my mom where I was going because she freaked out when she came home and couldn't find me. My grandmother called and told her I was with her, but that type of information coming from my grandmother didn't really make my mom feel any better. She got herself so worked up and angry over the fact that I was hurting so much that she went into the market and yelled at Dean for being such a jerk. That's when she discovered the reason we had broken up—because I didn't respond when Dean told me he loved me. Since I had remained fairly mute about why we had parted ways, this was news to her and she felt a little foolish having just scolded Dean. But that helped her realize that maybe this fear of commitment was yet another trait I had gotten from her and she decided to really try the thing with Max, which was good.

So they were now officially a couple and I was officially still broken up with Dean. And to be honest, I kind of missed him.

And then I found the box. It was morning and Mom and I had been chatting in the kitchen before school and work, which was a little difficult since Luke was hammering loudly on the roof.

Luke had been over a lot lately, fixing the porch railing, repairing shingles on the roof, fixing the porch railing again, and many other things that I couldn't even begin to pretend to know what I was talking about. So when Mom went out on the porch to holler at Luke, and I ran to the closet to get my school jacket, it slipped off the hanger and landed right on top of my Dean box.

I couldn't believe it. But it was absolutely my box. The skirt from my dance dress was peeking out of it. I stood in the hallway holding the box.

Mom came in and saw me there. I'd never seen her look more guilty.

"Ah. The Dean box," she said.

I didn't say a word.

"Okay. I know I was supposed to throw it away," she continued, "but . . . I couldn't. I mean, you're young and your head's all weird and you don't have any perspective because of that whole young weird-headed thing. So just please listen to me before you get mad. You're going to want that stuff one day. When you're old and married and looking back and thinking I certainly had an interesting life. And then, you can pull out all your old boyfriend boxes. Which is good because I threw away stuff I'd kill to have today. Look, I put it in with the Max box, so they could chat and keep each other company and commiserate about how they both had a Gilmore Girl and lost a Gilmore Girl and . . . sorry."

I didn't say anything. I just reached up and kissed her on the cheek. "Thanks."

Then I carried my Dean box to my room and shut the door. I sat down on my bed and opened the box. One by one I pulled out the contents.

The blue dance dress Mom made me.

Colonel Clucker.

The yellow box of cornstarch.

The bracelet.

I stared at the items, remembering why each went into the box.

∽

I met Lane after school that day and we were walking down the street, Lane grabbing fries out of the tray I was holding. She was chattering away.

But I wasn't hungry or talkative. I was thinking.

". . . and what I wanted to say was, 'Janie Fertman, you are a vacuous bimbo who will be turning letters as a profession one day, and the only way you'll know which letter to turn is when it *dings* and lights up, and I have no desire to stop and talk to you, ever!" Lane grabbed another couple of fries. "But what I said was, 'What, Jane?' And then she goes, 'You're cheerleader material.' Cheerleader material! Just like that. I couldn't believe it! I almost went full Matrix on her."

Lane stopped and stared at me. "Have you heard a word I've said?"

"Nope."

"I resent that. I'm a witty conversationalist."

I'd stopped walking and we were in front of Doose's Market. I stared at the door.

"What?" Lane said.

I smiled resolutely. "I'm going in."

"You can't."

"I'm going in."

"It's Thursday afternoon."

"I know."

"He works on Thursday afternoon."

"I know.

"We're talking you-know-who."

"I know."

"Oh my God!" Lane screamed when she finally realized what I was saying.

"Calm down."

Lane started jumping up and down. "Oh my God!"

"You're making a spectacle."

"You're getting back together with Dean!" she said, still jumping up and down.

"If you keep jumping like that, I'm going to videotape it and send it to Janie Fertman as your cheerleader audition," I warned.

She stopped jumping, but she was still bouncy. "When did this happen?"

"Nothing's happened," I stressed, glancing at the door. "I don't know what I'm doing exactly, or what he's thinking, or if he's burned all my letters and pictures or whether he hates me or what, but . . ." I took a deep breath. "I'm going in."

"I *do* encourage this," Lane said. "I love you, but you've been mopey and dopey and about twelve other melancholy dwarves for the past few weeks and I miss the old Rory."

"I miss the old me too."

"And I've been feeling bad for the new Rory."

"Well, she's staging a comeback."

"And may it be more successful than Peter Frampton's."

"Wish me luck."

"Luck!"

I took a deep breath, straightened my skirt, and walked in.

Once inside, I started to get nervous. I glanced at the checkout counter. No Dean. I looked around, but still no Dean.

Maybe I should just leave. I glanced out the window and spotted Lane peeking eagerly inside. I waved her away.

I strolled down an aisle, still looking for Dean. I picked up a can of black olives and pretended to study the label while I still looked around, then set it back down.

"Rory!"

The voice completely startled me. "Oh, Taylor. You scared me."

Taylor scowled at me. "What are you doing? You're walking around like . . ."

"Like what?"

"Dare I say, a shoplifter?"

I felt a blush coming on as I thought about the box of cornstarch. "Oh, I'm not here to shoplift!" I said a little too brightly.

"Well, you currently fit four of the eight characteristics," Taylor pointed out.

"I do?" I said nervously.

"You're alone. You look nervous. You're meandering in an aimless fashion. And you're wearing a baggy coat."

"Oh, I tend to run cold," I explained.

Taylor frowned somewhat suspiciously. "So what are you here for?"

"Oh, I'm looking for your checkout boy," I said. "I had a question, and I didn't want to bother you."

"Well, he's stacking on six." Taylor called around the corner. "Over here, please."

This was it. I swallowed and gathered my courage.

A short, geeky boy in glasses suddenly appeared.

"Mikey, this is Miss Gilmore," Taylor introduced us. "She needs some help. Take care, Rory." But as he left, he whispered loudly, "Watch her."

"Yeah?" Mikey asked.

"Uh, hi," I said, totally taken off guard. "I was just wondering . . . do you like working here?"

Mikey squinted at me. "Wha—?"

"I mean, do you enjoy the whole box-boy trade as a profession?"

He shook his head. "No."

"Okay. No. Good. So I'm just going to cross that off my list. Thank you for your time."

I turned and quickly went out the door.

Outside I started walking, fast. Lane had to run to catch up with me.

"Well?" she asked.

"He's not there."

"But he always works Thursdays."

"Well, I guess now he's taking Thursday afternoons off." I walked faster. "That's not good."

"How is that not good?"

"That means he's moved on."

"What are you talking about?"

"Obviously he's met one of those Thursday after-noon girls."

"What's a Thursday afternoon girl?"

"They're those slutty girls that get guys to switch their Thursday afternoons with another checkout guy so that they can go do slutty Thursday afternoon things," I said irrationally.

We crossed the street. "Okay, you're reading way too much into this."

"I shouldn't have gone in," I muttered.

"It was *good* to go in."

"Taylor thinks I was casing the place. Like I would ever shoplift there."

"You have shoplifted there," Lane pointed out.

I stopped on the corner and turned to look at her. "Lane, I'm going to ask you a question, and I want you to be more honest with me than you've ever been in your life. Have you ever seen him with another girl in school?"

"No," she said without hesitation.

I eyed her dubiously. "Lane . . ."

"No!"

"You'd tell me, right?" I pressed.

"Yes!" Then she frowned, worriedly clutching her hands in front of her. "No, I wouldn't, because it would break your heart, but I haven't."

"You swear?" I asked. "On the life of the lead singer of Blur?"

"On the soul of Nico, I swear to you that I have not seen Dean with another girl."

I sighed and let it go. "Okay."

We started walking again.

"He's miserable," Lane commented.

"Fine."

"And," she added, "in desperate need of a haircut."

I grinned at her. "Thank you." We passed Grant

playing his guitar, sitting on the steps in front of the church. I guess seeing Dean would have to wait for another time.

∿

The next day at school Tristin intercepted me at my locker. As I got out my books, he leaned back against the lockers and studied the cutouts of famous women I'd put up on the inside of my locker door. Emily Dickinson, Virginia Woolf, Colette . . .

"You should decorate this thing," he said.

"I have," I pointed out.

"I mean, with something other than a bunch of dead, black-and-white women."

"So, like what, curtains?"

"You know what I mean. I did mine up."

I laughed. "Yes, I've seen it. The naked picture of the Siamese twins is particularly classy."

Tristin held up a couple of tickets, one in each hand. "Know what these are?"

"They look like tickets."

"To P. J. Harvey!" he boasted.

I was a little surprised. "Wow, you've got good taste. I'll give you that."

"You're into P. J. Harvey, right?"

I glanced up at him. "Yeah. How'd you know?"

He grinned. "I'm all-knowing."

"How godlike of you," I responded.

I turned back to my locker, but then he held out a ticket and said softly, "One of these is for you."

"Oh, I don't think we should go to a concert together."

"Reason."

"It would seem like a date," I stated.

"Well, it would seem like a date because it would be a date," Tristin said, laughing.

"I can't date you, Tristin!"

"Well, I give you permission."

"And on that humble note . . ." I slammed my locker and walked away.

As I rounded the corner, I ran into Madeline, Louise, and Paris.

"Oh, Rory. Favor. Big one," Madeline said. She grinned and pointed at herself. "Look at the face."

"Sure, what?" I asked.

"Can I get your biology notes from Tuesday? I was out."

"To lunch," Louise added.

"Sure," I told Madeline. "They're at home. I can bring them later."

"Thank you, thank you, thank you . . ."

"One more and you're done," Paris said, cutting her off.

I continued on to class.

∽

When I got home that afternoon, I decided to try the Dean thing again. I changed clothes and headed toward his house.

I made myself walk up the sidewalk and stand on the porch. A cheerful hand-painted "Welcome" plaque dangled on the front door. I took a deep breath and mustered up the courage to knock.

The door swung open and a little girl poked her head out. "Hi."

So not what I was expecting. This must be Dean's little sister.

"Oh. Hi. How are you today?"

The little girl smiled. "Fine."

"Good, good." I glanced around.

"Are you here to see my brother?" she asked with a smile.

"Oh! No, no, not at all," I said, completely losing my nerve. "I'm, uh . . . I'm with the Girl Scouts."

"I'm going to be a Girl Scout someday," the little girl confided. "I'm a Brownie now."

"Oh, well, good. That's an excellent stepping stone."

She glanced at my jean jacket, black pants, and sneakers. "So, where's your uniform?"

"Oh, we're not doing uniforms anymore." I covered. "We're trying to blend in, you know, relate to the average person better. It was a very successful strategy for the Hare Krishnas, so . . ."

She squinted at me and studied my face. "You look like someone."

"I do?"

Then she smiled. "You're the girl in the pictures."

"What pictures?"

"The ones Dean has in his room."

My heart skipped a beat. "Dean has pictures in his room?"

She giggled. "There's a funny one of you sticking out your tongue. He had a lot."

"Wait, wait. 'Has' or 'had'?"

She was confused. "What?"

"You went from 'has' to 'had.' That's a big difference."

"It is?"

"Yeah." I bent down so I was the same height as her. "What's your name?"

"Clara."

"You're a pretty girl, Clara," I said.

She looked cautious. "Thanks."

"Now, was it 'has' or 'had'!" I asked.

She looked startled. "I don't know."

"You do know, Clara," I insisted. "'Had' is past tense, 'has' is present. Now *think*."

"I'm trying!"

"Can you go to his room now?"

"He doesn't like me in his room."

"Sneak in!" I urged her. "He'll never know."

Clara's face suddenly crumpled.

"Oh, no, no, Clara, don't cry!" I tried to soothe her. "I didn't mean to make you cry. I'm a nice person. I'm a Girl Scout."

Suddenly I heard a voice calling from inside the house. "Clara?"

Dean!

"Bye," I said quickly. I was halfway down the block before Dean could see who was at the door.

I hoped.

ꝏ14

The following night Mom and I took Max to Miss Patty's where the infamous Stars Hollow town hall meetings take place.

I smiled at them as we walked down the street. I liked and admired Max, and I liked how Mom looked when he was around.

"Hey, are you sure you want to go to this?" Mom asked him.

"You've been talking about these town meetings for months," he said. "I have got to see one for myself."

"Well, they're never dull," Mom said.

"And if you're lucky," I said with a smile, "some crazy lady will start throwing French fries at people she disagrees with like last time."

"So, were they cold?" Max asked Mom.

"No," she responded. "I was full."

"Oh, I forgot." Max dug around in the big bag of junk food he was carrying. "One for you," he said, handing something red to Mom. "And one for you." He handed me the same thing in purple.

"What are these?" I asked.

"Those are rings, and the diamond is actually candy so you can eat it."

"Max," Mom said, "that's very sweet, but we're not eight."

Then behind his back, Mom motioned to me.

"What's yours?" she whispered loudly.

"Grape," I said. "Yours?"

"Red."

"Trade you!"

"Yes!"

Max laughed. And we hurried inside.

The place was already packed, with several people standing along the back and sides. Some kind of debate was under way.

"Enough, enough of this arguing!" Taylor Doose was shouting from the podium. "It's time to put this to a vote. Okay, let's see a show of hands. All those in favor . . ."

A few people raised their hands.

"Oh, rats," Mom griped, "it's already started." We looked around for a place to sit.

"All those opposed . . ."

Dozens of hands went up.

Mom stood in the aisle and raised her hand, adding her voice.

"Lorelai," Taylor groaned, "you don't even know what we're voting on."

"Yeah, but I'm agin' it!" Mom said in a high country twang.

Several people laughed. Mom was always the same at these assemblies, yet Taylor never seemed to get used to it.

Max was already enjoying himself, I could tell. I had a feeling it was going to be one of our more exciting town meetings.

Taylor sighed dramatically. "All right, the nays have it. Let the record reflect."

Then I spotted Dean sitting in the back row, with his sister beside him.

He must have known I was there, with Mom getting so much attention, but he avoided looking at me.

Mom spotted some seats up near the front and shoved Max up the aisle ahead of her. I ducked my head and hurried past Dean to follow them, feeling Clara staring at me as I passed.

"Lorelai," Taylor called out, "I hope that's not food in that bag. Food is not allowed at town meetings."

"No, Taylor," Mom assured him as we took our seats. "It's, um, diapers for the little ones."

"The *what?*"

"Dorsal fins in Cucamonga," she continued.

Taylor turned to Miss Patty, who was seated just behind the podium. "What did she say?"

Mom leaned over to explain to Max. "I confuse him till he loses his train of thought and then he moves on. Hot dog?"

"All right," Taylor was saying. "I'd like to open the meeting up for miscellaneous issues."

"I've got an issue," someone called out, raising his hand in the front row. It was Grant.

"Who are you?" Taylor demanded.

Grant stood up. "The town troubadour."

Taylor scowled. "The *what?*"

"You've seen him, Taylor," Babette shouted from behind us. "With his guitar?"

"Ri-i-i-ight. The guitar," Taylor said scornfully.

"He plays on all the street corners," Miss Patty added.

"He *loiters* on street corners," Luke corrected from his spot two seats over.

"We're two peas in a pod, Luke," Taylor said.

"A scary thought, Taylor," he muttered.

"Go on, honey," Babette encouraged Grant.

"Thank you." Grant stood up before the crowd, shoving his retro black glasses up on his nose. Maybe he did look a little scruffy with his tousled brown hair and thrift-shop plaid jacket. But his street-corner music had become a part of our lives, and I for one enjoyed him being there.

"I've been the town troubadour for six months now," Grant began, "and I think I've done a pretty good job, and then"—he pointed angrily at a guy sitting on the front row—"*he* shows up."

The man he was pointing to was tall and lean with long stringy blond hair and glasses. The man squirmed a little in his seat, but waved shyly to the crowd. "Hi."

"And there's no room for a second troubadour in Stars Hollow!" Grant declared.

"Clearly," Morey interjected from the crowd.

Taylor was beside himself. "This is hands-down the silliest thing I've ever heard!"

"Hear him out, Taylor!" Mom shouted, holding out her hands in exasperation. "It can't hurt." Unfortunately, she had a fast-food bag in one of those hands.

Taylor glared at her.

"Uh, these are not fries," Mom said. "They're . . . Fahrfunugen Dugan Soogan."

Max nearly choked on his soda, he was laughing so hard.

"I opened the floor for issues of *substance*," Taylor argued. "This does not qualify."

"Don't be uncool, Taylor," Morey called out. "Music *is* substance."

"Watch it, Morey. After the anatomically explicit epithet your wife yelled at me earlier, you're *both* on probation," Taylor responded.

All this would have been very entertaining on a normal night, but I had other things on my mind. From my aisle seat, I tried to glance back surreptitiously at Dean, but caught him staring at me. I tucked my head and quickly turned around.

"All I'm asking is that the town troubadour laws be enforced," Grant argued.

"There *are* no town troubadour laws!" Taylor insisted.

"There ought to be something," Miss Patty spoke up.

"I've got the town handbook right here," Kirk called out.

"I don't get this, people," Taylor ranted on. "This man is practically a vagrant. I mean, where do you even live? What do you do for a living?"

"I don't want people to know these things," Grant said, clearly shocked.

"Why not?" Taylor demanded.

"Because," Grant explained, "that's part of being a troubadour."

"*What's* part of being a troubadour?" Taylor prodded.

"The mystique!" Grant replied.

"Oh, this is absolutely ridiculous!" Taylor appealed to the new troubadour guy. "Do you subscribe to this 'troubadour mystique'?"

The second troubadour shrugged. "I run a Kinko's in Groton."

"See, that proves it!" Grant said indignantly. "He doesn't respect the code! You're not supposed to talk!" He turned to his competitor. "You're not supposed to run a Kinko's. You're supposed to speak through your music. That's the whole point."

"What's your scam, buddy?" Taylor said, interrupting Grant.

"My scam?"

"Because if you are using the fine people of Stars Hollow to make a quick buck—"

"Oh no, Taylor," Miss Patty interrupted. "He doesn't accept money. I've tried."

"He may not now, but he will," Taylor warned. "This troubadour act is a moneymaking scheme. Why else would he be doing it?"

Suddenly I jumped to my feet and all my feelings tumbled out of my mouth:

"Because sometimes you have something you need to say, but you can't because the words won't come out or you get scared or you feel stupid, but if you could write a song and sing it, then you could say what you need to say and it would be beautiful and people would listen and you wouldn't make a complete idiot out of yourself. But all of us can't be songwriters, so . . . some of us will never be able to say what we're thinking or what we want other people to know we're thinking, so we'll never get a chance to make things right again. Ever."

I stopped to take a breath and realized what I'd done. I had never spoken at a town meeting before. Mom usually said enough for both of us. The entire room had fallen completely silent. Even Grant had dropped into his seat right in front of me to listen. Everyone was staring at me, waiting for what I was going to say next.

I gave Grant a light slap on the shoulder. "So . . . give the guy a license!"

I sat down.

I couldn't believe what I'd done. I'd made a total fool of myself.

But then the room erupted into applause.

Mom slipped her arm around me, clearly surprised. "Well, I liked your little speech."

And from the back of the room I heard Dean's little sister say, "That's the Girl Scout."

I sank down in my seat, wishing I had something to crawl under.

"Okay, in the interest of not talking about this subject for another second," Taylor announced, "I hereby designate 'Mystique Guy' over here the official town troubadour. And no other troubadour may usurp his territory, meaning this other guy."

With that, the meeting broke up.

People got up and started walking out of Miss Patty's. I glanced back at Dean, but his chair was empty.

∽15

On Monday morning as I crossed the campus to class, I spotted Madeline.

"Oh, hey, Madeline," I called out, hurrying to catch up to her. "I've got those notes you wanted."

But she just kept walking, without turning around. "No, thanks."

"No, these are the ones you asked for," I clarified. "The biology notes from Tuesday? The other day, you said you—"

"No, thanks."

"But . . ."

She ran off.

"What's wrong with her?" I asked Louise as I came up beside her.

Louise shrugged. "Nothing's wrong with her . . . Mary."

"Mary?" I groaned. "Oh no, not this Virgin Mary

thing again." That's what they used to call me when I first came to Chilton.

"Not virgin," Louise corrected me. "Typhoid."

She walked off too, and then Paris appeared, glaring at me.

"What?" I said.

"You know, when we met at the beginning of the year, I didn't like you," Paris said, "because I thought you were some rube from the sticks, and I have no patience for rubes."

"How very enlightening," I said.

"But then I discovered that you're not so dumb. You even seemed modestly interesting at times. That's when I made a very big mistake: I let my guard down. That won't happen again."

"What is all this about?" I said.

Paris paused to face me. "It's about using people for your own sick ends. It's about making enemies where you should've made friends."

"How did I make you my enemy?"

"Oh, I think you know." She started walking off again, and I followed her.

"What? Was it setting you up with Tristin? I'm sorry about that. I thought I was just being nice."

"Oh, sure you did."

"I helped you get ready," I reminded her. "I loaned you my mother's clothes, which I still haven't gotten back, by the way."

"Oh my God, you're right! I hope those weren't the ones Skippy had her puppies on. I'll check when I get home."

"Tell me what I did!" I said as we went inside the building.

She ignored me.

"Paris!" I shouted, grabbing her arm to stop her.

She turned and glared at me. "Think about it at P. J. Harvey!"

And then I realized what had happened. "Is that what this is about? I'm not going to P. J. Harvey."

"Tristin says you are."

"Well, then, he lied."

"I saw the tickets."

"He bought those tickets on his own," I insisted.

But Paris just waved me off. "Look, I'm over Tristin, so don't back out on my account."

"There's nothing to back out of."

"I don't have time for extra things like concerts anyway," she said, walking away again. "I'm already lining up my extracurricular activities for next year. By the way, are you still going out for the school paper?"

"You know I am."

"You're going to need a faculty recommendation."

"I think I can swing it."

"And the support of the student editor."

"I'm not worried."

Paris smiled. "I just got the job."

"Oh. Congratulations."

"Thank you. And don't worry. You'll have some role. How's covering the new parking lot landscaping sound?"

"Peachy."

"Too bad I already filled the slot for music coverage," she went on. "You know, record reviewing and such? You'd have been perfect for it. I gave the job to Louise."

"Louise owns two CDs!" I protested.

"Yeah." She smiled smugly. "Well, gotta go." She started up the steps to the second floor, then turned to glare down at me, with Louise and Madeline just be-

hind and flanking her like they were the witches of
Eastwick. "Have a really great summer," she said before
they all turned and walked up the stairs.

I stood there, staring after them.

&

After school, Tristin stood outside waiting for me. I ignored him and walked past, but he followed.

"So I'm a little tired of this game," he said as he fell
into step with me.

"What game?" I snapped.

"Are we meeting there, or what?"

"What are you talking about?"

"The concert's tonight," he reminded me.

"Well, I hope you and the empty seat next to you
have a lot of fun," I replied.

"I'm starting to get a little irritated, here."

"So am I."

"What are you mad about?"

I turned on him. "You've been telling everyone that
I'm going to this thing with you!"

"Just a couple."

"You told Paris," I said. "Paris and I had just started
to get along and now she hates me again."

"Well, if the damage is done, you might as well go to
P. J. Harvey with me."

"Never," I said firmly. "Never. I am *never* going anywhere with you, *ever*."

He started to get mad. "You know, these tickets cost
me a fortune."

"They cost your *daddy* a fortune," I shot back.

"I don't even know anybody else who's even into this
stupid guy!" he snapped.

"P. J. Harvey's a woman," I corrected.

I turned and started to go, but then he snatched my books from my arms.

"What are you doing?" I exclaimed in disbelief.

"I'll give them back when you agree to go with me," he said, pleased with this new tactic.

"You're pathetic, Tristin. Keep the books. I'm leaving."

I continued on, Tristin quickly following. Then I froze.

I couldn't believe what I saw.

A green truck was parked in the drive and a guy was leaning against it, waiting. "Dean?" I said to myself. I rushed toward him.

He stood up as he saw me, but then he saw Tristin behind me and shook his head, disgusted.

"Dean! What are you doing here?"

"Leaving," he snapped.

"Don't go," I said.

He yanked open the door to the truck, but I slammed it shut.

"I shouldn't have come," he muttered.

"No, wait!"

"I feel like an *idiot*!"

"*Why?*"

Finally he faced me, his eyes filled with hurt and anger. "Because I come all the way out here and I see you with *him*!" he shouted, jabbing his arm toward the school. "That's just great."

I looked where Dean was looking.

Tristin stood there, holding my books.

"No, Tristin was just—"

"I don't care!"

"No, listen—"

"He's got your books, Rory!"

"But he took them and he wouldn't give them back! Please, just tell me why you're here."

Dean threw his hands up, frustrated, and walked away from me. "I don't even know."

I followed him. "Yes, you do!"

He whirled around. "Because I thought . . ." He looked at me, he looked at Tristin. "Forget it."

"No, say it!" I insisted.

"I thought you were trying to talk to me."

"Oh."

"I mean, you came to my house—"

I cringed. "That wasn't me."

"It *was* you."

"It must have been someone who looked like me."

"My sister recognized you from the pictures in my box."

I blinked. "In what box?"

"The box of stuff I have of us. Pictures and letters and everything I got from you."

"You have a Rory box?" I asked softly.

"And what was going on at the town meeting?" he continued. "All that stuff about writing a song?"

"I—I don't know what I was talking about . . ." I stammered, shifting uncomfortably.

"So, that had nothing to do with me?" he asked.

I opened my mouth, but the words wouldn't come.

"Well, I must have imagined it all, then."

We both stood there, not knowing what to say.

When I didn't speak, Dean shrugged and motioned to Tristin. "Your boyfriend's waiting," he said, disgusted. And he headed for the truck.

"He's not my boyfriend!" I called after him. "I hate him!"

"Whatever," Dean said as he opened his car door.

"Dean!" I called out desperately.

He hesitated, but didn't turn around. "What?"

"Stop!"

"Why?"

A simple question. But why couldn't I give him the simple answer?

Say it! I screamed inside my head. *Say it—before it's too late!*

I took a deep breath and climbed up on top of a scary mountain—and jumped.

"Because I love you, you idiot!"

Dean turned around and headed straight for me. And then he was kissing me, for all the world to see.

❧

Mom left me a message to meet her at Luke's at seven. Big news, she told me. But she wouldn't tell me exactly what. Something about yellow daisies. And Max.

I was so happy over what had happened with Dean that I couldn't imagine bigger news, but I also couldn't wait to see her. Couldn't wait to tell her my news, too.

But Dean and I had spent the whole afternoon talking and I lost track of time.

Now it was dark, and I was late. I raced through town toward Luke's and I felt like I was in a dream. The town was sparkling from the recent rain, and the lights on the trees made everything look magical. Except I knew I wasn't in a dream; it was better, because it was real.

I passed Grant, who was at the curb officially being the town's troubadour, and I sent Mom a message to her pager to tell her I was almost there. As I rounded the corner, I saw Mom rush out of Luke's.

Then she saw me and we both stopped where we were. My eyes filled with tears as I grinned at her. And when she saw my face, she, too, broke into a smile.

Then we ran toward each other, right down the middle of the main street of Stars Hollow. And when we finally met, we grabbed each other's arms, and we were both laughing and out of breath and talking at the same time.

"He just—"

"I just—"

"You first!" we both said at the same time.

"I told Dean I love him."

"Max asked me to marry him."

And then we were laughing and screaming and jumping up and down, and all I could think about was how beautiful life was, and how wonderful it was to live in Stars Hollow, and how lucky I was to have Lorelai Gilmore for my mom.